# SHORT STORIES OF BALLARD

## Gary Brose

CC Productions
4005 20th Ave West #133
Seattle, WA 98199

Edition #1

**ISBN:** 9781790488988

Published by CC Productions - December 2018

# TABLE OF CONTENTS

# Author's Foreword

The inspiration for *Short Stories of Ballard* came to me during a warm October day as I strolled around the many streets and avenues near Market Street. As often as I do that, I still find myself marveling about how many cool and unique stores, eateries, bars, and other sites we have here all within walking distance.

After my wife, Kathleen, and I moved from Magnolia to Ballard in 2010, we explored often and both enjoyed the rich history we have here and the wide variety of places to go and things to see.

I've written four business books and seventeen novels (under a pen name), and I wanted to write something about Ballard too. Another "sites to see" type book seemed less than inspiring, so I pondered on it for a while. Lately, I've been reading more about short stories and how challenging it is to write one. In a full-length novel of 150,000 words, the writer has many pages to flesh out the characters, lead up to inciting events, and build the tension to a thrilling conclusion. A short story, especially one of three thousand words or less, allows for almost none of that.

An author by the name of O. Henry is arguably recognized as the father of short stories. He was famous for his surprise endings, such as the one in "The Gift of the Magi." Reading that is a humbling experience for any first time short-story writer. I'm humbled too, but I tried my best to keep the stories light and interesting and still squeeze in a twist or two.

I hope you enjoy your read and don't be too surprised if you find your neighbor weaved into the fictional storylines.

# DRESS FOR SUCCESS

It was still raining. November in Seattle was like that, and for some reason, Amy Cutter was convinced that Ballard got more than its share. Being cooped up in her apartment on 24th Northwest was starting to drive her mad. She was itching to get out and breathe some fresh air.

She considered her options and decided to stay put for a while longer. It was supposed to clear up, so she chose to trust that the weather forecaster was right about that call.

******

Down the street from where Amy lived, Carly Dane parked on 24th and waited for the rain to lighten up long enough for her to dash out of her car and get into the Lemon Drop Boutique on the corner of 59th. The liquid sunshine continued to pour down, and for a brief moment, she wanted to believe it was an omen. *Maybe I'm not supposed to do this. It might be better to turn around and go home,* she thought. *I really don't want to part with this dress…so many memories.*

Carly no sooner finished the thought than the downpour obviously lessened. She grimaced and gathered her courage. *I'm here. It's time. I have to do it.* Grabbing the parcel on the passenger seat, she glanced in her rearview mirror, opened the driver's door, and slipped out.

Five seconds later, she entered the boutique and said, "Hi, Jodi."

Jodi Obde, the proprietor, waved, smiled back at her regular customer, and moved behind the counter to see what she had for her this time. They chatted a bit for five minutes. During that time, Carly twice considered returning the money and asking for her dress back.

Ultimately, she accepted the proprietor's offer, gave up her parcel, and ran back into the rain.

******

Amy stood staring out the north side window, watching the downpour. It looked like the rain was finally letting up, but as soon as she was certain of it, it started coming down harder again. She pursed her lips and went into the kitchen to fix some tea.

This was the time she enjoyed the least. Amy knew she was stalling. It was the Thanksgiving break at her company. A two-day work week and then three off in a row. Thanksgiving had been spent with her cat, Misty, and a single serving of turkey loaf, whole cranberries, and a glass of Riesling. Misty got her usual cat food. Now, today was Friday and being trapped inside was driving her crazy. She knew why—she knew where her mind was going to go.

Seated in the kitchen nook, Amy stirred her tea. *I'm forty-three years old and here I sit alone, two short-term loves and too many meaningless flings later. It's clear I'm going to need some kind of magic to change all that. My only family is my brother, and he lives two thousand miles away. I have a decent job, but everyone I work with is married or committed. Turnover is nonexistent, and the next time I meet someone intriguing at work will be the first time. OK, that sounds harsh, but let's be real, I'm not going to meet anyone there who could…*

Her thoughts trailed off, as she couldn't bring herself to finish the statement. Amy tried to always stay busy. She worked forty hours a week, volunteered at Adams Elementary, and attended the Business Improvement Area meetings of the Ballard Alliance, but it was starting to appear pointless. She felt invisible anywhere she was. *I have a better chance of running into an eligible man at the grocery store,* she thought.

Finishing her tea, Amy resolved to think positive and terminate today's ruminations. Glancing outside again, she was happy to see the rain had let up. She picked up Misty and, looking her in the eyes as though the cat understood every word she spoke, said, "You be good. I'm going out to meet the man of my dreams."

Laughing at herself, she set Misty back down, put her coat and beret on, and left, locking the door behind her.

"First I'll go to the grocery store and scout for dinner, then I'm going up Market and window shop a bit. This is a big sales day, right? I might see something I really like," she said to herself as she exited the apartment complex and took a left toward Market Street. An older woman passed her, eyeing her suspiciously, as Amy realized she had been talking to herself quite loudly.

It didn't matter. She was outside in a light rain and getting some fresh air. She wasn't going to let herself be embarrassed by anything she did. She continued down the east side of the street, passing NW 60th and then 59th.

Amy stopped a moment and looked in the window of the Lemon Drop Boutique, spotting a dress in the display that caught her eye.

Inside she went, smiling at the woman behind the counter.

"See something you like?" Jodi asked.

Pointing back toward the display window, Amy replied, "I like that yellow dress with the crocheted trim, but it looks a bit small for me. Got any others like that?"

Jodi came around the counter and took another glance at the dress in question. "It's sort of one of a kind. I don't think I have any more that shade or style exactly. I'm not sure—" She hesitated for a moment, then continued, "You know, I just got one in moments ago. I know the woman who dropped it off, and she's about your size. She said it was a favorite of hers, but she just couldn't keep it any longer."

"She outgrew it?" Amy asked.

"Well, in a manner of speaking. I think it still fit her fine, but her husband of twenty years passed away and, well, I think he must've really liked it too. She didn't want to give it up, but she just couldn't wear it anymore."

Amy stared back at the shopkeeper impatiently, as if to say *Well, let me see it!*

Snapping out of her reverie, Jodi pulled a slightly wet package off a shelf behind the counter and unwrapped it.

"It really is gorgeous," Jodi blurted out as she loosened the string holding the paper around it.

Amy's heart pounded more quickly, and her eyes widened as she looked at it for the first time. It was an elegant, blue evening dress with subtle flower imprints on the lower half. It looked to be very close to her size and likely to hug her hips just a bit, which was an instant plus as far as Amy was concerned.

"Oh, it's lovely!" Amy exclaimed. She held it up to herself and immediately asked, "How much?"

Stumbling a bit, Jodi replied, "Well, I just got it in and haven't even had time to have it cleaned or anything. I was thinking I'd probably price it the same as the yellow one in the window."

"Sold!" Amy replied as quickly as she could. "It looks perfect. Smells like it was just washed. I've been looking for something like this for a while." She handed her credit card over to the store owner, smiling all the while.

Jodi processed the card and stared back at her.

Always a quick study, Amy asked, "Is there something wrong? You look like you were about to add something."

Recovering quickly, Jodi shook her head and said, "No, it's nothing. I'm Jodi, by the way."

Amy introduced herself and they talked for a few moments about the joys and the trials and tribulations of small business ownership.

Clutching the parcel tightly, Amy said her good-byes and darted out the front door, anxious to get home and try the dress on. As she glanced up above at the threatening skies, she stepped in front of a man rapidly walking south. He slammed into her and spilled his coffee all over Amy's coat and her parcel.

Amy let out a shriek at the same time he did, and they both stumbled back. The parcel slipped from her grasp, falling into a shallow puddle. The man stared back at her, regret written in his eyes.

Amy sized him up quickly. He was midforties, about six feet, handsome in a subtle kind of way.

"Oh, jeez, look what I've done!" he said. "I am so sorry. Is that something you just bought at the store here?"

Amy nodded. "Yes, I was just going to go home and try it on."

"Look, it was my fault. I wasn't watching where I was going. Let me pay for the cleaning. Oh, and for cleaning your coat too. There's the Sparkle Cleaners I use right kitty corner from here. I insist. Let me at least take care of that for you."

"Well, that would be nice of you," Amy said. "I'll take you up on it."

Inside, Jodi watched with horror as they collided and with interest as something appeared to spark between them. She watched them cross the street to the dry cleaners, and then, chuckling to herself, she returned to her duties.

Fifteen minutes later, Amy stopped back in to the store. Jodi was with another customer but excused herself to see what Amy wanted.

"Are you OK?" Jodi asked.

Amy smiled back and said, "More than OK. I'm getting my new dress cleaned and a lunch date too. I just came back to ask you what it was that you didn't tell me before."

Looking around a bit, Jodi said, "I told you, it was nothing." Even as she said it, she couldn't hide a hint of a smile.

"That's your story and you're sticking to it?" Amy asked playfully.

"I, um, I don't like to tell stories out of school. I try to protect my customers' privacy."

"I get it," Amy agreed. "I just thought, you know, that it might have had something to do with…well, never mind."

Amy turned to leave, but Jodi caught up to her.

"This one time, I think my other client would find it amusing and would want you to know."

Amy nodded, "What was it?"

Jodi looked around and continued in a quieter voice, "The woman who dropped it off said she was wearing that dress the night she met her husband for the very first time. She, um, well, she said it was like magic."

Amy locked eyes with her for a moment and asked, "Only children believe in magic, right?"

Smiling a secret smile, Jodi said, "Of course. Of course."

# PAYBACK

Cort knew he had just enough time. He caught the elevator on the sixth floor, exiting at the lobby level of the VIK condos. He passed by the front desk and gave a quick wave to Jim, the facility manager.

*No time for chit chat,* he thought. *I've got my data to pour over and enough time to get a dark roast coffee and a treat at Sip and Ship.*

Cort opened the front door and took a right toward twentieth, south a block to Market Street and left another hundred feet to the nearest coffee house. In no time, he was in line at the Sip and Ship. As he waited, Cort reached back for his wallet. It wasn't there. He checked his jacket pockets and came up empty. Reaching into his front pants pocket where he always had a roll of dollar bills, he pulled out two Kleenexes and a flash drive.

Considering his options while the woman in front of him finished paying for her order, he overheard her last comment. "Thanks, Sue. See you tomorrow." Then she turned and exited with her carry-out items.

Cort stepped up and went through his planned charade. He gave his order for a latte and a chocolate chip cookie, and the young woman finished ringing him up.

She looked up to him and said, "Five eighteen."

Continuing the farce, Cort reached for his missing wallet, checked all his pockets for her benefit, and said, "Um, you know, I left in a hurry and forgot my wallet." He laughed, hoping she would be amused too. Sue's face was unchanged.

"Look, I just live up the street. Maybe you've seen me before. If I can have this now and pay tomorrow, I'm sure—"

Cort stopped as he saw Sue shaking her head.

He felt a tap on his shoulder. As he turned around, a woman standing in line behind him edged her way past, flashed her debit card over the scanner, and said, "Sue, add my usual order to his bill and I'll cover it."

It all happened so fast, Cort had no time to protest. Not that he would've. Cort nodded to her, took his coffee and cookie, and headed to a large picnic table where an older woman was already seated.

"I need some room to spread my papers out, so I'm going to sit here, OK? You look like you're ready to leave anyway."

The woman with the near empty coffee cup looked up from her book and said, "Make yourself at home." If Cort had actually been listening to her, he would have caught the whiff of sarcasm, but Cort really rarely listened to anyone.

He nodded as if he had listened and proceeded to spread his paperwork out all over the table as he sat down to study the printout and see if the computer program he'd designed was working as he hoped.

After a few minutes, he looked around the room and caught a few nasty stares. *What's their problem? Oh, jeez, the snowflakes are probably upset that I didn't thank that woman properly. I did thank her. Didn't I? Well, I'll cover my butt and do it again now.*

He walked over to where the woman was seated. She seemed to be enjoying the time, gazing out the window, watching people go by.

"Excuse me. I wanted to thank you again for what you did," Cort said, loud enough for others in the area to hear.

One old man nearby blurted out, "Nice try. You never thanked her the first time."

Shuffling his feet and looking around nervously, Cort acted like he didn't hear that and said, "Here's my card. If you give me yours, I'll be glad to reimburse you."

The woman took the card and noticed his name and title. "Not necessary. I'm happy to do it."

Taken aback, Cort replied, "No, really, I'd feel better if I evened it up. Just give me your card. I could send that to you tonight. Do you take bitcoin?"

Several people listening nearby nearly choked on their drinks.

The woman rose from her seat and picked up her paper cup. "I have to go. If you reimburse me, it kind of ruins the whole thing." With that, she squeezed behind another patron's chair and headed for the door."

"Wait!" Cort yelled. "Wait. I didn't get your name."

"And you're not going to," the old man said, laughing. Others joined in. Cort stood there a moment and considered running after her, but he couldn't leave his printouts lying out there for anybody to see or steal. He returned to his table, appetite ruined. Taking one last bite of the cookie, he picked up his papers and left.

Walking back to the VIK, he thought, *That was really rude of her. I mean, I showed her my card. Cort Linley, a fine name showing class, and my title, Head Programmer, TellTale Project, DigiTime Inc. I mean, how could she not be impressed?*

Three days later, Cort returned to the Sip and Ship and sat in a corner, nursing his coffee. He had an unobstructed view of the front door, and he watched as people came and went. *If she shows up, I'll give her a ten-dollar bill and make sure everybody sees it. Practically double what she paid. That'll redeem me.*

She didn't show that day, nor the next. People started noticing the programmer, always sitting in the same spot at that same time of the day, waiting and watching. After a week and a half, on a sunny Thursday, he finally grew weary of the exercise and gave up. It was only four thirty in the afternoon and a programmer worked all kinds of hours. He headed back to the office at South Lake Union.

Entering the office again at five in the afternoon, he passed by Quinn's desk. She looked up from her programming project and said, "Cort, you're back. Working some odd hours lately, aren't you?"

Cort smiled back at her and agreed, "I guess so. How are you doing?"

"Good," Quinn replied. "Actually, that was going to be my question for you. Are you doing OK?"

"Sure. Why?"

Quinn checked around the room to see if anyone else was paying attention to them. Everyone seemed self-absorbed as usual. "Well, you, um, just seem different lately."

"Different? Like how do you mean?" Cort asked.

"Well, I don't know. Kind of, um, nicer, I guess," Quinn said quietly.

Cort mulled that over and replied, "Something happened that made me rethink a few things. I mean, I'm, you know, just trying to sort a few things out."

Quinn stared back at him. "OK, well, for what it's worth, you seem less intense and less angry lately. It's kinda nice."

"I've been thinking about some other stuff, you know?"

Quinn eyed him. "You mean, like…like nonwork stuff?"

"Yeah. Don't tell anybody I said that, OK?"

Quinn smiled to herself, feeling like she had just learned something that no one else in the world knew. "Your secret's safe with me. So what happened to you?"

"Long story. Maybe I'll tell ya someday," Cort answered, then flashed her a mysterious smile.

He worked until ten that night and left a note for Quinn asking if she was free for dinner tomorrow night. Then he headed home. As he drove across the Ballard Bridge, he thought, *I've got the authority to work my own hours, but even so, people are wondering why I always leave at three o'clock each day. I give up. All this for a pretty short conversation anyway. What was it she said again? If you reimburse me, it kind of ruins the whole thing. What the hell does that mean? How could getting money ruin something?*

The next evening, Cort relaxed with Quinn at the Pasta Bella restaurant on Fifteenth. He told her about the strange woman who paid for coffee and a cookie for a complete stranger. He explained how he couldn't fathom her motivation.

Quinn listened quietly, and after a few moments, she said, "Maybe you should try it yourself. You know, see what it feels like. You might like it."

Cort shook his head. "What's in it for me? I pay out some money and get nothing back. I don't get it."

As their evening ended, Quinn brought it up one more time. She said, "Cort, I enjoyed our meal together. Thank you for asking me to join you, but you know what I enjoy more?"

"No. What?"

"I enjoy when you show your softer side. When you're not such a hard charger all the time. And I think you should explore it more, if, you know, you're brave enough."

9

"What's bravery got to do with it?"

Quinn eyed him and said, "You have to be brave to do something for someone and not stick around for the credit. I think there's more satisfaction if you don't expect something in return."

Recognizing a challenge when it was tossed in his face, Cort flashed a smirk and replied, "Maybe I will. Maybe I'll do something way bigger than what *she* did. I'll keep you informed."

Three days after the dinner with Quinn, he got up at five in the morning and headed to work. Shooting down Fifteenth with virtually no traffic, he turned up Mercer Place, continuing to think about the chance event at Sip and Ship. Talking out loud to himself as he drove, he repeated it again. "If you reimburse me, it kind of ruins the whole thing." Finally, as he said it the hundredth time, he realized he knew what it meant. He knew she was just one of those kind of people who didn't value money as much as kindness and friendship, and she simply enjoyed doing things for others.

He thought about the other Ballardites in the coffee house. The older woman who he ignored and shoved his way into her space. The man and others who laughed at him when he said he didn't get her name. *Am I that clueless? I'm not, am I? I have an important job. I have to hurry and get right to the point. I can't be someone who sits around and sips coffee while they're not working. I saw her. She was just sitting there with a smile on her face and watching people through the window. Who has time for that?*

During the next week, Cort worked long hours and thought more about the unusual woman who paid his bill and asked nothing in return. He thought about her silent, placid smile as she watched people go by. *What does she know that I don't?* Slowly a plan formed. By the end of the week, he knew what he would do.

On Saturday morning, he walked into the Sip and Ship and pretended to look at the menu. When no one else was in line or within earshot, he went to the register and encountered Sue, waiting on him again.

"What would you like?"

Quietly, Cort said, "I'd like a hundred dollars' worth of coffee."

"Excuse me?"

"Here's my debit card. Charge a hundred dollars to it, and when the next customers come in, give them whatever they order for free and deduct it from the hundred. You know, kind of a surprise."

The young woman let a small smile escape her lips, then she recovered and was all business once again. She processed the bill and said, "OK, it's done. You want anything?"

Cort looked at her and thought, *OK, I'm trying this out. I want to know why she did what she did and seemed to enjoy it.* "Um, no, no, that's it. I don't need anything. I think, you know, that in Ballard, this is what people do, right? Anything else would kinda ruin the whole thing."

Giving him a knowing smile, she thanked him, and he left.

About halfway through Cort's meandering walk back home, he caught himself smiling. Trying hard to analyze his feelings, he considered his deed, talking out loud as he walked. "OK, that was weird. Kinda fun, though. I wonder who walked in there and got a wonderful surprise. Maybe I'll do this again. Like, maybe I'll pick a different coffee house every month and drop a hundred bucks and see if it's still fun. I think I will."

He walked a little farther and had one more thought. *Quinn is kinda nice. No one ever said I have a soft side before. I'll tell her all about what I did and she'll be impressed.*

He took another twenty steps before it hit him like a wrecking ball. Cort stopped in the middle of the sidewalk, forcing other pedestrians to walk around him. *OK, jeez, I get it now. I can't tell her. I can't do this so I get recognition or so she's impressed. I have to just do it for me. I have to keep it to myself. Otherwise…it kind of ruins the whole thing.*

# LATE LIFE LESSONS

"You're late," Martin deadpanned.

"Nope, you're early," Alex countered.

Alex took a seat next to his friend. They were both in their winter coats, bundled up tight against the December cold.

"Is that from Vera's?" Martin asked, pointing to his friend's coffee cup.

"Sure is. I like their coffee," Alex replied.

"I thought you liked their bacon and eggs?"

Alex looked at his aged friend and shrugged. "I do. Just because I like their coffee doesn't mean I can't like their bacon and eggs too."

Martin smiled, knowing it didn't take much to get his friend riled.

Alex and Martin were both in their midseventies, and every Monday, Wednesday, and Friday for the last three years, they had met at the old Bell Tower Park on Ballard Avenue. Alex was the taller of the two, and he still had a full head of hair, all of it silver. Martin's head was shiny. His four-year-old granddaughter described him as having bald hair. He always wore an Italian flat cap to keep his head warm. There were only two benches at the small park, but they always seemed to snag one of them before anyone else. Of course, they met at seven thirty each morning, and demand for bench space was traditionally low at that time.

Today they scored their favorite bench—the one facing 22nd Avenue Northwest. They liked the view better, and more than anything they liked watching all the people walk by going to work, heading home or out to eat, or just getting exercise. The intersection at 22nd and Market had one of the highest walking scores in the country, and there was rarely any shortage of people to watch.

Neither Alex nor Martin were loquacious fellows, but they were never short on opinions. Their comments were consistent, brief, and sometimes brutal.

Two fortysomething women walked south on 22nd toward Ballard Avenue on the other side of the street. As they passed in front of the Tides and Pines clothing store, Martin nodded his head slightly in their direction and said, "The tall one, she's a looker."

"And the short one, she's got some virtues too. I like her," Alex added.

"You don't even know her," Martin countered.

"There you go," Alex said. "Trying to ruin the moment. I do know her. Look at her clothes—sensible and not flashy, but she looks good all the same. And she smiles a lot. How can you not like somebody that smiles all the time? Her eyes kinda sparkle too."

"You don't even have your glasses on. You can't see clearly that far."

"Always the naysayer," Alex replied. He smiled to himself. This was the routine. If he didn't have it to count on, he wouldn't know what to do.

They sat in silence for a while, and when Martin's coffee was half empty, he set it down on the ground and lit up his cigar.

With no comment, Alex did exactly the same. He crossed his right leg over his left and made himself comfortable. Martin crossed his legs too.

"There he is." Martin nodded again toward the sidewalk on the other side of the street.

"Mr. Bowler Hat. Look at him, sauntering down the street like he didn't have a care in the world."

"I bet he's not the sharpest tool in the shed. Just kinda strolling along."

Alex agreed with Martin. "Yup, I doubt he's got a job."

Satisfied that they had nailed another one, they sat quietly puffing on their cigars.

"It's eight ten," Alex announced.

"Where are they?"

"Running late. Both of 'em. I find it strange that—"

"Hold your horses," Martin whispered, interrupting his pal. "Here comes Little Miss Sunshine now. Always a stylish walk, that one. But she looks like always, like the kindest young lady you could ever meet."

"Maybe we *will* meet her someday," Alex suggested.

Martin laughed. "Oh, yeah, that would be the highlight of her day, wouldn't it? Getting a chance to meet two old geezers like us. What a thrill for her."

Not disagreeing, Alex called out, "Look. Right on time. There she is, the Wrathful Wonder."

"Oh, man, she is a sour one, isn't she?" Martin made a face like he was tasting a lemon.

"She'd be hell on wheels to work for. I bet she hasn't got any friends. I don't know, she just looks unhappy every day as she walks past. And it still seems strange how she and Miss Sunshine always show up at the same time but don't even know each other."

They sat on the bench together for another hour, drinking their cold coffee and enjoying a second cigar. At nine fifteen, without saying another word, they both shared a look and rose from the bench at the same time.

Alex looked at his friend and said, "Well, I guess we got 'em all pegged again."

"Right every time as usual," Martin agreed.

They both turned and went their separate ways.

******

Wednesday was a virtual repeat of Monday as they commented on every passerby, remaining consistent in their assessments of the pedestrians who dared to invade their corner. At nine fifteen, Martin rose and said, "Got 'em all pegged. No one's fooling us."

Alex patted his friend's shoulder and said, "We're always right. We know what's going on in Ballard."

******

Friday and a sky full of dark clouds came around as Alex arrived first and claimed their bench for them.

Martin arrived thirty seconds later from across the street.

"You're late." Alex said it matter-of-factly.

"You're early," Martin countered. He looked at Alex's coffee cup. "You got that at the Bible and Coffee Shop. I thought you liked Vera's."

"Too busy. If I had waited in line there, I would have been late by a minute. Can't have that. Besides, they make a mean cup of coffee over there too." Alex nodded toward the shop across the street. "Where'd you get yours?"

"Ballard Coffee Works on Market. They like me up there."

"I doubt it," Alex ventured. "You're a curmudgeon. Maybe they just pretend they like you."

"No, I'm pretty sure they like me. I just have black coffee. Nothing hard about that. I don't complicate their lives by asking for a double mocha super-duper skim latte with cinnamon or something."

Alex smiled. Martin did too.

And then it began.

They commented on everyone that passed by, then the two fortysomething women walked by together as usual.

Martin nodded his head slightly in their direction and said, "The tall one, she's sure a looker."

"And the short one, she's got some things going for her too. I like her," Alex added.

"You say that but you don't even know her," Martin countered.

"There you go," Alex said. "Trying to ruin my day. I know her type. Look at the way she dresses—doesn't spend lots of money but gets some real bang for her buck. She's not flashy, but she looks good all the same. And she smiles a lot. You gotta like somebody that smiles all the time, right?"

Martin sat quietly for a moment. Then he said, "You forgot to say something about her sparkly eyes."

Alex shook his head. "There you go. It's kinda dark today, so I couldn't see her eyes and didn't see if they sparkled or not. I don't make this stuff up. I just call it like I see it."

Stifling his laugh, Martin said, "OK, just checkin'. Don't get all riled up over it."

"I wasn't and—hey, look. Here comes the Wrathful Wonder."

She was walking on their side of the street this time, and as she neared them, she looked over, smiled, and started to walk their way.

Alex and Martin glanced at each other as if to say, "What's up with this?"

"Gentlemen, hello!" the Wrathful Wonder said. "I see you out here often. Here, please take this. Our new restaurant, Sienna's, is opening this weekend." She handed them each a flyer advertising the opening of a new restaurant on Ballard Avenue. "We're having an open house lunch today at one o'clock. It's free, and I'd love it if you two would come by. I'd so like to meet you and have some time to learn all about you."

She smiled broadly at them, nodded, and headed back down 22nd.

Tongue tied, Alex and Martin sat in silence.

"She was nice. Maybe we got her wrong," Martin volunteered.

"Hard to believe, but—hey, here comes Little Miss Sunshine," Alex said, cheering up.

No sooner had he said it than she looked right at them and stopped in her tracks. She stormed on over toward them and pointed her finger in their faces. "You think I don't see you. Every day you're checking me out as I walk past, and I'm here to tell you to knock it off. You guys think any girl walking by is someone you can comment on. Well, not *me* anymore. You got it? If I hear one more peep out of you two, I'm going to come over here and introduce you to Mr. Fist."

Alex's jaw dropped. Martin's eyebrows lifted to his hairline. They both nodded.

She unfolded her fist, gave them a dirty look, and left.

Again they sat in silence for a few moments. Finally, Alex asked, "That was Little Miss Sunshine?"

"Maybe she got up on the wrong side of the bed," Martin suggested.

Nodding, Alex mumbled, "I guess."

They broke out their cigars, crossed their legs, and tried to regroup. They said nothing at all for the next thirty minutes.

At nine o'clock, Mr. Bowler Hat walked by.

"There he is," Martin said needlessly. "Look at him, what a lollygagger. All the time in the world. Not a care at all."

Alex, getting back into form, said, "I bet he's not the brightest bulb in the pack. Just taking his time. Nowhere to be."

Martin agreed, "Yup, I doubt he's got a job."

Satisfied that they had nailed another one, they sat quietly puffing on their cigars.

# DOWN ON HIS LUCK

It was five thirty in the afternoon on a cold December day in Ballard. The coffee at the Mighty O hit the spot for Harry Lyman. With the temperature in the low forties, he needed something to warm him up and give him a boost of energy as well.

He downed his last swallow and exited, walking east on Market Street. Harry reached into his pocket and felt the realistic-looking black .45 toy pistol he had hidden there. *I can't afford a real gun and got no intention of hurting anybody anyway. But these are desperate times that require desperate measures.*

Harry was fifty-eight years old and had been unemployed for two years. He used to work in a clothing shop, supervising the crew that was creating a now-defunct brand of outdoor wear. He was good at his job, and he enjoyed it. So much so that he spent nearly thirty years of his life working for the Staley Outerwear Company. One Monday morning a little over two years ago, he showed up for work along with the morning crew and found the doors locked and the business dark. A sign on the door said *OUT OF BUSINESS.*

No warning, no hints that there was financial trouble. Nothing. A few months later he learned that Ron Staley, the owner, had never funded the pension plan and was six years behind on paying payroll taxes. He apparently cleaned out the bank account and left the country.

Now Harry's unemployment insurance had run out, he wasn't old enough to start taking social security, and the nearly two thousand a month he expected from his pension would never happen. No one wanted to hire a going-on-sixty middle manager, and here was Harry walking down the street with thirty-seven cents in his pocket.

*Not even enough to buy one of Mighty O's delicious donuts.* His brain understood but his stomach was in full revolt.

Today he was going to cross the line. No one would give him a job, so he had to take desperate action if he was going to have anything to eat today. Today he was going to rob a store and treat himself to a fine meal. If he was lucky, he'd have time to eat it all before the police arrested him.

*Yeah, and if I'm real lucky, I'll get killed and put out of my misery.*

Harry looked around at the donut shop. He could do it here, but there were a lot of people, including some little kids. He didn't want to upset anybody, especially kids, so he decided to move on and find a store with fewer customers in it.

Harry turned around and walked down the south side of Market Street coming upon Palermo Pizza and Pasta, just west of 20th Avenue. He'd had a chicken marinato pizza there once a few months ago and promised himself he'd come back and have another. Now, he walked in and planned to make a bit of small talk while he sized up the place. Entering the front door, he moved inside and found himself third in line to get a table. He realized he'd probably arrived during their peak hour—the place was packed.

A young woman came forward, flashed a pleasing smile, and welcomed a party of four. She guided them to one the few remaining open tables, then returned, still smiling as she greeted an older woman standing alone. "Mrs. Hansen, just one today?"

"No," the older woman said. "My husband is parking the car and will join me in a moment."

The hostess replied, "Oh, good. I'm so glad you're here tonight. We have some great specials. I've got your favorite table open. Come this way."

She returned a moment later and looked at Harry. "Welcome! What can I do for you?" she asked, beaming her smile at him so strongly that he felt as though she had saved that one up all day just for him.

"I, um, I mean, no thanks. I, uh, I changed my mind."

He turned and left the restaurant. Another couple was coming in at the same time, and he held the door for them, earning a sincere thank-you.

*That wasn't a good place to rob. That young lady was so kind and nice. I didn't want to ruin her day.*

He continued on down to Ballard Avenue and strolled down the street. He passed several restaurants that were too busy and held too many people. He spotted a retail store selling antiques with only one customer inside. *Too few customers. He may not have a lot of money in the till. I'll pass.*

He reached Hattie's Hat, an established bar and restaurant, famous in Ballard. This was it. Not too many people, and he knew they were normally busy enough to have some cash. He walked in and took a seat in one of the booths near the door.

A waitress appeared almost immediately and handed him a menu. The woman smiled at him and said, "Oh, hi. Welcome back to Hattie's. I know I've served you before, but I can never remember names. I'm Darla."

She looked back at him, fully expecting him to introduce himself. He nodded and gave a half-smile back in return. "I'm…I'm Harry."

"That's right. I remember now. Harry, good to see you again. Start you off with some water and maybe a cup of coffee?"

Harry pressed his eyes closed and shook his head. "I, uh, I'm sorry. I changed my mind. I have to go."

Rising quickly, he charged for the door and disappeared into the street.

*I remember her. Heck, I had a bowl of soup here last week and she waited on me. What are the odds of that? I can't go robbing people I know, especially when they're that nice.*

His stomach growled again, and Harry steeled himself to make another try. He walked farther down Ballard Avenue just a few steps, he entered a store he hadn't been inside before. Almost instantly, he realized it was an outdoor gear store. He stepped back out for a moment to see the sign outside. It was called Gold Dogs. He recognized the name as a former customer of his old firm. Something about that seemed to fill Harry with greater resolve. *This is the one. This is where I'll do it.*

He stepped in and started looking around. A man approached him and asked, "Can I help you find something?"

"Um, no, I'm just looking," Harry replied. *I'm keeping conversation to a minimum here.*

"I'm Ryan Goldsmith, my wife and I own the store. We have some great new jackets that just came in if you're looking for something a little warmer than what you have on," he said, pointing to the west wall of the room.

Barely looking at him Harry shook his head. *Why does everybody in Ballard have to be so damn nice?* He glanced over at the wall with the jackets and was drawn to them. Forgetting why he was there for just a moment, he walked over, pulled the hanger and jacket off the hook, and took a closer look. It was a product from the Staley Company. "I remember this style. This is well made," he muttered to himself.

Ryan was right there and he quickly agreed. "Very well made. Unfortunately, the supplier went out of business and I think that's one of the last ones we have from them. Would you care to try it on?"

"Um, no," Harry mumbled.

"How about this one? This is made by a new supplier, and we really think they have a great product," Ryan said.

Not able to resist, Harry felt the fabric and said, "I know these guys. They *are* good. Good material, really keeps you warm and retains the heat. Sleeves are a little puffy for my tastes, but I know a lot of people like that. Good price too."

Ryan shuffled back a step or two and sized up the customer. "You know about this stuff?"

As Harry was about to answer, two young men came into the store and split up. The first one walked directly toward Ryan while the other went straight to the flannel shirt rack.

While Ryan was engaged with answering a series of questions from the first man, Harry eyed the other one.

Without warning, the second young man grabbed a handful of flannel shirts, still on their hangers, and ran for the door. Before Ryan could extricate himself from the man's accomplice, Harry, still a spry man at fifty-eight, ran after the thief, yelling "Hey, you, stop!"

The young thief turned to the left outside the front door and ran down NW Vernon Place. A large group of ship workers was ending the day and walking up to Ballard Avenue, blocking the fleeing man's way. He turned around and looked at Harry, judging his chances to be better with one old man.

"Drop those clothes!" Harry ordered.

The young man dropped them immediately, reached into his pocket, and pulled out a switchblade, which flew open. He waved it at Harry and said, "Get out of my way, you old man!"

Harry sneered at him and said, "I'm not having a good day, and now you've made it worse." He pulled the toy gun out of his pocket and said, "You drop that little toothpick and lie flat on the ground or I'm gonna show you what a bad day really looks like."

A crowd of people on the other side of Vernon Place cut off his only other escape route. He twisted his head around and saw everyone closing in on him. He dropped the knife and lay down on the ground as instructed.

Harry quickly put the gun back in his pocket and watched as the shipbuilders came up and put their heavy boots on the man's back, holding him in place. Ninety seconds later, the Seattle police showed up and carted him away.

Ryan came out and retrieved the shirts. He looked at Harry and said, "Thank you! I mean, really, *thank you*! That was something. Are you OK?"

Embarrassed by the event, particularly knowing why he was there in the first place, Harry just nodded and tried to slip away.

Ryan moved quickly to grab Harry at the elbow and steer him back into the shop. "His friend did everything he could to block me from getting to the door, but I guess they didn't count on you. Anyway, you can't leave yet. I've got a gift award for you."

Harry protested, but Ryan insisted. "We keep them for special events and this qualifies, believe me." He searched quickly through a few drawers but couldn't find what he was looking for.

Harry, his hands shaking, mumbled, "I gotta go."

Ryan looked him over again, a little closer this time. His clothes were dirty and he looked as though he had slept on the street that night.

"You had anything to eat lately?" Ryan asked.

Harry shook his head and tried again to leave.

Not ready to allow that, Ryan again took Harry by the elbow, walked him out the door, and led him down the street. They entered Hattie's Hat. Ryan looked around and spotted Darla, a familiar face—one of the waitresses.

Signaling her over, Ryan said, "Darla, this man is hungry and I owe him a reward for helping us stop a robbery just now."

Darla nodded. "I heard all that action out there." Shifting her gaze to Harry, she said, "Sir, you are welcome here. Why don't you take a seat in this booth?"

"Whatever he wants, Darla," Ryan said.

Harry sat down as Darla seemed to materialize a menu out of thin air.

His stomach growling as he perused the menu, Harry looked forward to a filling meal for the first time in days. He ordered a house salad, the Guinness Meatloaf, mashed potatoes, corn bread muffins, and a hot coffee. The coffee came immediately, and while waiting for his meal, he had to wipe away the tears twice.

*I almost did something unspeakable. What was I thinking? I'm going to learn from this and I'll find some help somewhere. I just—*

His private thought was interrupted when he noticed Ryan still standing at the table. "I didn't catch your name, sir," Ryan said.

"It's Harry. Um, Harry Lyman."

"Harry, you enjoy your meal. Darla will send me a bill—just eat what you want. But I have one question for you. Back in the store, you showed you have a knowledge of outdoor wear. Just wondering, you wouldn't be looking for work, would you?"

"Well, I…yes, I do need a job. I'm afraid I didn't make a very good first impression today. These clothes are—"

Ryan cut him off. "That's an easy fix. I have an opening for a sales associate and I don't come across experienced applicants very often. Since I already know I can trust you in a pinch, and well, I'm feeling lucky. Could you start tomorrow?"

"I could…I, uh, I'd be honored to work at your fine store," Harry said.

Ryan slapped his thigh and said, "I am one lucky guy! Come on by at ten o'clock, OK?"

"I will, sir," Harry began. "But I think *I'm* the lucky one today."

# LOGAN'S LOSS

Logan Crane sat on the balcony level at MacLeod's, a Scottish restaurant and pub on Ballard Avenue. He was twenty-eight and a lawyer at a downtown Seattle law firm on the fast track toward partnership. He stood a healthy six-foot-two, a hundred eighty pounds, literally with eyes of blue, a dark black wave of perfectly combed hair, an eye-catching countenance, and seemingly everything going his way. He sipped his scotch while he enjoyed periodic stares from some of the women on MacLeod's second level.

He took a second to glance back at a particularly cute brunette who was eyeing him and flashed an engaging smile. As he turned back to his drink, his buddy, Roger, showed up.

"Hey, there's da man!" Roger called out, taking the seat across from him.

"How you doin', buddy?" Logan said.

"I'm good. What's it been, two months?"

Logan nodded. "Almost. It was when we played basketball with the guys in Lynnwood."

"Oh yeah. I remember. I was the star, as usual," Roger added.

"Oh, yeah, you sure were," Logan said, laughing. "What did you score that night? Three points? And my team won. I *always* win, remember."

"I always try to forget the final score. And no, it wasn't three points. I tied my all-time high, thank you, pumping in one basket after another, scoring four points."

"My mistake," Logan admitted. "Four points, that's some record!"

Roger laughed along with Logan.

A waitress came by and brought a bourbon-and-seven Roger had ordered on the way up the stairs.

"So you scored some tickets to the Mariner's game tonight for me?" Roger asked, getting to the point.

Handing them over, Logan said, "These are like gold, man. Terrace Club level. Perfect first base side view. Front row on the aisle. Just for my buddy, Rog."

Roger took the two tickets and said, "Thanks, Logan. I sure am glad you're not a baseball fan. I look forward to getting these once or twice a year. Now if only I had a hot girlfriend to take with me."

"I'm nearly all powerful, but no one could make that happen. Remember, you have to have some bucks and be good looking to get a chick. You're oh for two there," Logan jibed, a devilish grin on his face.

Roger downed his drink and started to rise from the table. He wanted to come right back with a snappy retort, but it eluded him. A second later, Shannon appeared at his side, poked him on the shoulder, and said, "Roger, good to see you again. What are you doing here?"

Shannon Ray was twenty-six, a bright young legal aide at the same firm where Logan worked.

"Hey, hi, Shannon," Roger replied. "I was just meeting up with Logan to get some tickets he had. Hey, want to go to the ball game with me? I know you came here for your date with this ugly guy, but this is your chance to slip away with me."

"Ooh, a baseball game or a hard Rock-a-Billy concert at the Tractor. Two tough choices. Sorry, I guess I'll stick with this ugly lawyer here."

"Your loss!" Roger said, laughing. "Hey, Loag, thanks again for the tix, I'll be sure to—"

"Hold on a second," Logan said, interrupting. He held his right index finger in the air as he answered his phone. He listened for twenty seconds, then said, "Tonight? Really? It can't wait until the morning?" He listened again, then rang off. "Sorry, bad news. I gotta go back into work."

"But I just got here. You have to go now?" Shannon asked.

"No, not right now," Logan said. Then he added, "I could stay here all night if I didn't want to be partner. But I do, so duty calls. I'd offer you the Tractor tickets, but I know both of you aren't hard Rock-a-Billy fans. Why don't you go to the ball game together?"

Deflated, Shannon looked at Logan as he rose from his seat and shrugged. "I'll miss you," she said as she planted a quick kiss on his mouth.

"Likewise. Wish it were different, but…" He let the sentence die away.

"I understand. Call me if you get done early, OK?"

Logan looked to Roger and said, "Rog, see you next week at the basketball game. Try and get on my team because…" He stopped talking, grinning at his friend, waiting for him to finish the sentence.

Roger was gracious and allowed him to have his fun. "Because your team will win."

Not satisfied yet, Logan asked "And why is that?"

Acquiescing, Roger added, "Because you *always* win."

Logan poked his pal in the chest with his elbow. "Don't forget it." He was chuckling as he descended the stairs and headed out the front door in a hurry.

Shannon excused herself to go to the ladies room and rejoined Roger at the front door.

"Rog, I'm sorry, but I don't think I'd be very good company tonight. I think I'll pass on the baseball game."

Roger nodded. "It's OK. I've got some friends I can call," he lied gracefully. "I'll walk you home. You live nearby, right?"

"Just a few blocks. Ballard has so much traffic now, I always walk. There's no parking anyway. Hey, where did you park?"

"No problem for me. I found a free spot about three miles west of Wenatchee and hiked on in."

Shannon laughed. "That close? Good for you."

"Thanks," Roger replied, chuckling along.

"I just live—" Suddenly she stopped walking. Checking her pockets, then her purse, she flashed a look of panic. "Oh, jeez! I must've left my phone in the ladies room. We have to go back."

Walking rapidly, they retraced their steps, and Roger waited outside as she reentered MacLeod's. A minute later she returned holding her phone up high. "Somebody turned it in to the bar. My gosh, I'm glad I thought of it when I did."

They started their walk back up Ballard Avenue. Glancing across the street, they saw a long line of people waiting for the hard Rock-a-Billy concert starting in thirty minutes. Suddenly, Shannon stopped in her tracks. She stared at the line across the street as Roger tried to see what she was looking at.

"That bastard!" Shannon said.

Roger saw it, too. Logan was standing in line with a very young and cute blonde in high heels and a miniskirt. He had his arm around her waist, and she was stretching up to whisper something in his ear.

"Oh, God. I knew it was too good to be true," Shannon said, in something above a whisper.

"Oh, hell. I'm sorry, Shannon. That's Logan. It's, well, it's just him being him. It's what he does."

Shannon pulled on Roger's arm and ordered, "Let's get out of here. I just want to go home."

They began walking again on the same route as before.

"Damn, I was kinda hungry too. I was looking forward to dinner after the show. Oh well, Rock-a-Billy isn't really my thing anyway. Not that that bothered Logan any."

"I could take you somewhere if you'd like," Roger suggested a bit too timidly.

"I thought you were going to the ball game?"

"Well, I don't want to leave you alone like this. You have to be a bit down and—"

"Oh, hell. Fact is, I think I'm relieved. I knew this wouldn't last. Logan always took me to these pricey places for entertainment or dinner, and I'm more of a simple girl. I don't need all that. I just like good conversation and good food, regardless of the price. I knew he'd burned through girlfriends like a forest fire through dead-dry kindling, but he's such a hunk and, well, it was fun while it lasted."

"You're not bummed?" Roger asked.

"Well, can't say I'm thrilled. That little skanky number he was with is who he preferred over me. That kinda hurts, but I'm still hungry. Where'd you really park?"

"I told you. Just west of Wenatchee," Roger replied, tongue firmly planted in his cheek.

Shannon laughed. "I always liked that about you, Rog. You can make me laugh. Where are you really parked?"

Roger suppressed a smile, but part of it sneaked out anyway. "I'm just off fifteenth at fifty-third."

"Oh, well, if you have to walk that way anyway, wanna take me to Ballard Brothers? They've got Mexican food as well as seafood now. I like it all."

Roger's grin nearly exploded on his face. "Now you're talking! I love the Ballard Bar and Grill—that's its new name. I always get the cod and chips there."

Twelve minutes of walking and chatter later, they arrived at the restaurant and placed their orders. Shannon experimented, getting the veggie quesadilla, while Roger got his standard cod and chips.

Staring at Roger's order, Shannon smiled and said, "Logan said that you always order the same things. He said you've had the same car forever, you wear the same jacket all the time, have the same job at the trucking company, you've lived in the same place. He calls you Mr. Boring."

"I prefer to think I'm Mr. Consistent. Either way, that's me. I find something I like and I just stick with it. Why change?"

Shannon eyed him. "You've really had the same job for all that time? You drive a truck?"

Roger took a sip of his beer and replied, "Well, I've worked at the same *company* since college, but not the same job. I drove to begin with, then they made me a dispatcher, and last month I took over as operations manager. I'm not devoid of ambition; I'm just, you know, not in the same league as Logan."

"But you've been friends since grade school, right?"

"Yeah, we were best buds, but things change and he was always a hard charger. He likes the fast lane. I'm kind of a middle lane guy. These days, we don't really have much in common, but we're friends. He thinks some of the things I do are stupid and I think some of the things he does are rude. We find a way to get along anyway."

"Like dumping his girlfriend in the middle of a date so he can go out with someone else?" Shannon said, her lower lip trembling a bit.

Roger shook his head and said, "No. That was more than rude. That was mean spirited. That was clueless. That was a terrible thing to do to anyone, especially someone as kind and attractive as you."

Shannon stared back at him. "You're not married, are you?"

Roger shook his head as he took another forkful of coleslaw.

"Seeing someone?"

Again Roger shook his head, his mouth full.

Shannon looked down at her meal for a moment, then slowly said, "You know that thing you said? That thing about once you find something you like, you stick with it?"

"Yeah?" Roger asked, his head turned to one side.

"So I get how that could go for cars, or jobs, or homes. Does that go for people too?"

Locking eyes with his dinner partner, Roger nodded and said, "Especially for people."

They ate in silence for a few minutes, then Roger stretched his usual boundaries of conversation and said, "In case you're wondering, not that I'm making a big deal out of it or anything, but in case you were wondering, I, um, I *do* like you. Liked you from the first time Logan introduced us."

Shannon smiled. "Well, I always thought you were the nicest friend Logan had."

Roger laughed quietly because he didn't know what else to do.

Shannon knew. She reached over, put her hand on his, and said, "Think we could still catch that baseball game?"

Roger nearly leaped out of his seat. "Are you kidding? I know all the best parking places. We could be there before the third inning starts."

"What are we waiting for?"

They left the restaurant, and Roger led the way to his car.

As they got in, Shannon leaned over from the passenger seat and gave Roger a quick peck on the cheek. "What do you think Logan would call *that?*" she asked, laughing.

Roger turned to her and said, "I don't know, but I know what I'd call it."

"What?"

Smiling broadly, Roger said, "I'd call it Logan's loss."

# SQUARE PEG

It had been four months since her grandmother died. Four long months, three jobs, and too many sleepless nights. Kagome was Sansei, third generation Japanese. Her parents had been born in the United States, but her grandparents were from the old country.

Kagome was born and raised in Seattle. Her parents had moved to Ballard when she was three and it was all she ever knew. Now, her parents were retired and living in Arizona, something she could never understand. How they could enjoy the heat was far beyond her.

Her grandfather died when she was eight, and her grandmother had lived with them since then. When her parents moved south, she and her grandmother stayed in the small two-bedroom home on NW 57th, just off 28th. The mortgage had been paid in full when her father sold their small restaurant for more money than they ever imagined they would get.

At thirty-one, Kagome occupied the house on her own now, after spending the last six years living with her grandmother and enjoying every minute of it. She held several jobs during those years, always in the restaurant business. She had been a bartender, a waiter, and, for most of her life, a cook—she specialized in Asian food but had worked in all kinds of restaurants and loved to cook anything. Mostly, though, she loved to cook for her grandmother. She would often work shifts in the midday, then come home and make a wonderful dinner for her and Grandma Shiori. Sometimes she'd make it at the restaurant and bring it home with her. They would eat together with soft music in the background, and her grandmother would regale her with story after story about life in Japan.

Today, she sat at their kitchen nook table and sipped tea by herself. The lights were off, the scents of dinner cooking were long gone, and no music was playing. Kagome sipped her tea in peace and pressed her eyes closed to stem the tears from falling.

"This is crazy," she whispered to herself. "I can't keep doing this. I have to move on with my life."

It was spring in Ballard, the time of year when hope springs eternal. The flowers were blooming, the morning rain was drying as the afternoon sun warmed the air, the Mariners weren't eliminated from playoff contention yet, and the sounds of mothers with strollers wafted in from the sidewalk.

Kagome put on her light jacket and walking shoes and headed out. *Gotta do something. Gotta find a job again—something that I won't quit after three weeks,* she thought to herself.

She walked to 24th, then Market Street, seeing all the same sights she had seen for nearly thirty years. New stores, restaurants, and bars had replaced the old ones, but there were no surprises to see. She passed some eateries she had worked for in the past, including the Matador and Palermo, two places she had already worked at in the last four months. Both were fine restaurants with some great people to work with, but after a few weeks at each, she ran into the same problem—apathy. Inevitably, she would reach a point where she asked herself, *What am I doing?* The work didn't fill her with joy or make her happy. *Why? It always has in the past.* She loved interacting with the guests and learning about them, treating the regulars with care and the new clients with a bit of humor to put them at ease, but she didn't feel like making jokes now. After a few weeks, she could see that she wasn't doing her best, and the moment she realized it, she gave her notice. She knew the restaurant deserved better, and she was certain she didn't really fit in.

Three jobs since her grandmother died, and she quit all three.

As she strolled down the street, she shook her head as if that would expel the thoughts that filled her mind and her soul. She meandered all the way to 15th Avenue, crossed the street to the east side, and turned left. Aimlessly now, she walked north.

A man and woman in their forties walked past her going the other direction. Kagome nodded and mumbled a hello. They did the same.

*All right, I'm getting my exercise in and my quota of social contact now.* She chuckled to herself. *Yeah, that was really knocking it out of the conversation park. I mumbled and they did too. This is crazy. I said that already, didn't I? I've got to snap out of this and find a job and live a normal life.*

She kept walking north, crossing 58th Street, and stopped in front of Saint Alphonsus Church. A worker was outside, pulling weeds out of the cracks in the sidewalk and by the stairs. He looked up just as Kagome stopped some ten feet from him, and she realized he was wearing a frock.

"Hi," he said with a smile. "I'm Father David. I just noticed all these weeds and decided to tidy up a bit."

Kagome laughed and replied, "Well, you're doing a pretty good job of it."

The priest chuckled, then stood and extended his hand. "Thanks."

They shook as she replied, "Glad to meet you. I'm Kagome Shimoda I, um…I was just out for a walk."

"I know. I saw you coming from a few blocks away," Father David said. "Looked like you were talking a bit to yourself. I like to do that, you know, when I'm walking and have a lot on my mind."

Catching Kagome by surprise, she stifled a sob and tried to respond, but she pressed her lips closed and nodded slightly.

"Anything I can help you with?" he asked.

Kagome, still struggling, managed a shrug of her shoulders.

Sensing she would not make the decision, Father David said, "Why don't you sit down with me for a minute." He gestured toward a bench on the church patio. "Tell me what's on your mind and maybe I can help somehow."

"I'm not Catholic, Father."

"Well, today's your lucky day. Pretend I'm just the wise old gardener. C'mon." He pointed again to the bench and led her up the stairs.

Seated facing west, Kagome poured out her thoughts to Father David for the next fifteen minutes, barely stopping to take a breath. He listened without interrupting. When she finally stopped, he looked her in the eyes and said, "I'm sorry for your loss. Your grandmother was obviously an amazing woman, and I can see why you miss her greatly."

Kagome nodded, unable to add anything more.

Thinking for a moment longer, the priest added, "So it sounds like you feel a bit lost—not sure how to gain back some meaning to your everyday life."

Kagome chuckled softly.

Smiling and exceedingly curious, Father David asked, "Did something about that strike you as funny?"

She nodded more vigorously. "Japanese names all mean something. Kagome means lost."

Father David leaned his head back and rolled his eyes. "I'm sorry."

"It's OK. I'm the one who's sorry. I've taken too much of your time already. I should go and—"

"Wait just a minute there, young lady. You can't go until the wise gardener has dispensed his wisdom. Do you want to hear it?"

Still chuckling a bit, Kagome nodded.

"I don't think it's the work that lacks meaning for you in your latest jobs," Father David began. "I think it's that you don't have anyone to share stories with, anyone to personally cook for, anyone to make happy like you did for your grandmother. And believe it or not, I just talked to someone at a Rotary meeting this morning who told us about *her* problem. And I had no answer for her then, but I think I do now."

"What is it?" Kagome asked.

Father David pulled out a small notepad and pen from his vest pocket. "I want you to do me a favor. Go to this address and ask for Mindy Byers. Tell her that you are an experienced chef and you know you could easily cook for and interact with her clientele."

"Actually, I don't have a culinary degree, but I trained under my father and others for years and they were all amazing chefs."

"If you trained under the best, you're a chef. Do it, Kagome. Go there. After she describes the job, you can decide then if you're interested or not. But you have to hear it, OK?"

"This address on Leary Way?" Kagome asked, trying hard to picture which restaurant it was. "I'm not sure I—"

"I'm sure!" Father said emphatically.

Kagome hesitated, then smiled back at him. "Well, you *are* the gardener, after all."

Father David laughed and agreed, "That's right! I am. Go now. She's works all the time. I bet she's there now."

Kagome thanked him for listening and headed toward Leary Way. Fifteen minutes later she was on Leary walking past El Borracho. She looked ahead and thought, *Full Tilt doesn't need a chef, does it? Maybe Porkchop and Company? No, still looking for 5433.*

Stopping at the doors now at the Ballard Landmark Senior Living building, she checked the address again.

"5433 Leary Way," she said out loud. "This is it."

Entering, she asked for Mindy Byers, and a minute later, Mindy came out and met her in the lobby. "Yes, can I help you?"

"You're Mindy?"

"I am," she responded matter-of-factly.

"Father David sent me. I'm a chef…an experienced chef," she blurted out.

"Are you looking for work?"

"Yes. No. I'm not sure."

Standing right there where everyone could hear, Mindy said, "Well, we're looking for an ace cook who can interact well with our clients and cook them a meal that makes them think they were already in heaven."

Kagome looked around the room and saw more than twenty pairs of aging eyes staring back at her, all waiting for her answer. The room fell deathly quiet.

Mindy tried to help her along. "Father wouldn't send you here if you weren't qualified. I lost my chef when he moved to Denver, and although we've brought in others to pinch-hit and they've done well, we need someone permanent. Do you, um, cook all kinds of food?"

"I've done everything. French, Italian, Mexican, American, and Asian, of course. I love cooking everything."

"Well, we have a rather urgent need right now. I have time now, if you want to go to my office for a full interview. We're looking for someone who will embrace the community. This is a different environment than a typical restaurant. You essentially serve the same clientele every night. You get to know them and they you. Do you think you might be looking for work at a place like this?"

Kagome swallowed hard and said, "Actually, no, I'm not." She stalled for a moment while she summoned up some courage. "I don't think I'm looking for work. I think…I think I'm looking for some meaning."

Mindy smiled and looked around the room at the residents as they listened in on the exchange. "You know, this isn't for everybody. It has to be kind of a special fit for you." She paused, then gave it her best shot at maintaining Kagome's interest. "Think you could find a way to fit in here?"

"I'm kind of a square peg."

Liking her refreshingly honest answers already, Mindy looked back at her and said, "That's perfect!"

Kagome nodded and gazed around at the crowd of onlookers. A kindly woman in her eighties shyly smiled at her. Two men shared a comment, then turned to her and gave her a friendly nod. Suddenly feeling a warm glow inside, Kagome said, "I think I'm finding some meaning here already."

# WHATEVER FLOATS YOUR BOAT

*Comma or no comma? C'mon, think, Maury. I say no.
Next. OK, here's another time I used* great. *Are you kidding me? I
can't come up with a better word than* great? *How about* amazing
*or* outstanding? *No,* awesome…*no. How about*…grand? *Yes,
that sounds like something this nerd would say.*

He paused for a moment and took a sip of his Coke.
He'd been nursing it for forty-five minutes, and most of the
ice was gone. Maury Woods looked around the room and
smiled to himself.

Olaf's Bar was his refuge. He came by often and
claimed his usual seat. All by himself, he'd sit at the large
round booth to the left of the front door. It was hard to
find a bar lighted well enough to allow him to read and write
easily, but Olaf's large front windows provided plenty of
light for the corner booth and a few other spots. Only big
groups wanted that corner, and they were rare on most days.
If the Seahawks were playing, forget it. Olaf's was packed
then. But today was a boring Monday afternoon in March.
Maury, sitting alone, quietly nursed his drink with his books
and notepads spread out while everyone else came in pairs
or more and were laughing and making all kinds of noise.
He smiled at the sight and wouldn't have it any other way.

Maury moved from Alabama to Seattle five years
ago. He settled in Ballard because that was the first place he
could find a room for rent that he could afford. Now he

knew he'd just been lucky. Ballard was a place he would be happy to live in for a long time.

Many times he chuckled to himself about how things turned out. Maury was black as coal and here he was in a nest of Scandinavian folks as pale as the moon. It never mattered to him, and he was delighted to see it never really mattered to anyone else either.

He landed his first job at the Brown Bear Car Wash on 15th and now held two part-time jobs as a waiter at the Hi-Life and the Ballard Annex Oyster House. He made good tip money and had moved to a studio at the Urbana Apartments three years ago.

But Maury's ambition wasn't to be a waiter. That just paid the bills. What he really wanted was to be an author. More specifically, he wanted to write the next great American novel. He moved to Seattle to get away from his family—a family that had other expectations of him—and to have as much alone time as possible that he could devote to writing.

Today, he was struggling with a scene in his latest effort. The protagonist had painted himself into a corner and was desperate to escape—without losing the love of his life, of course. He stared at the manuscript, trying to imagine how his main character could make that getaway.

*He can't just walk away and leave Callie waiting in the lurch. He can't go to the cops because—*

"Maury, you look like you need a little more ice," said Tom, the manager at Olaf's, as he approached the table.

Maury looked up, then glanced back at his Coke. "Yeah, I could. Guess I should drink more and chew ice less, huh?"

"Doesn't matter to me. You making any headway there?"

Maury shook his head. "My characters aren't cooperating."

Tom laughed and moved on to the table left of Maury's spot.

Maury realized that Tom was the only person he had talked to all day. *I gotta socialize more, even if I do suck at it. Meeting a young lady or two wouldn't break my heart either. Those two Latina ladies at the corner of the bar look awfully nice.*

He shook that off, dismissing the random thought, and returned to the task at hand. His character needed rescuing, and he was the man to do it.

*OK, think, Maury. And think faster too. Remember, Dad named you after Maury Wills, Dodger's shortstop who stole over five hundred bases in the major leagues. Not sure how that helps me, but c'mon, think faster.*

He stared at his manuscript and willed himself to start writing, but nothing was coming to him.

*This isn't me. I never get writer's block. I got these stories written in my head already. What's wrong here? So, he can't go to the cops. He can't go back to the mob again. He needs some ingenious plan, and my old one won't work now that I had him blow up his computer in the last chapter.*

Maury ran his hands through his hair and rubbed his chin, grimacing as he struggled. *I've got to figure out how to—*

"Maury!" Tom bellowed out. "Wake up. You've got company."

Eyes widening, hair disheveled, Maury raised his head and saw the two Latinas standing three feet away from him. The shorter one had a beer mug in her hand while the taller one held a mug in each hand.

"You looked like you were struggling hard there, and we thought maybe you needed a beer break," the shorter one said.

Tongue-tied, Maury bumbled through an incomprehensible sentence: "Can't, um, you couldn't…I mean I couldn't, didn't see you." He stopped before he made it worse. He shook his head back and forth quickly, laughed at himself, and said, "Sorry, I'm out of practice. Please, sit down and join me. Is, uh, one of those for me?"

The two women laughed and quickly took a seat.

"Yes, here you go," the taller one said as she passed a mug over to Maury. "I'm Pilar. This is Theresa." She pointed to her friend.

He smiled back, not sure what to say next.

"Oh, Pilar," Theresa said, looking at her friend. "It's so sad. He must not have a name."

Pilar feigned sadness as Maury laughed and jumped in.

"Sorry. I'm Maury." He held out his hand and shook both of theirs.

They both laughed. Pilar said, "We know. Tom says you always sit at this corner. You're the writer who camps out here and agonizes over every word you write."

"I don't agonize over *every* word. Just some of them," Maury said, chuckling.

"Well, you were sure struggling for the last ten minutes," Pilar said. "We kept peeking at you, and you looked like your best friend had just left town. You were writhing and thrashing around like you were in a battle to the death."

Theresa leaned forward and said, "So we thought you needed a break from all that agony."

"Yeah, what are you writing, anyway?" Pilar asked.

"I'm trying to write, um, well, the great American novel. Something that will be groundbreaking in literature. Something that generations to come will appreciate. And something that, you know, sells like hotcakes too."

All three of them laughed.

"Is this your first novel?" Theresa asked.

"No. No, I'm afraid this is my eighteenth," Maury said quietly.

Following up on her last question, Theresa asked, "What happened to the other seventeen?"

Pilar shot her a look, and she immediately regretted asking it.

Maury defused their concern. "They were like practice for this one. I hope. At least, that's what I tell myself. I learned a lot writing those, and I think, you know, every mistake made makes me a better writer in the long run. I'd say my earlier books were sitting at Amazon collecting dust, but eBooks don't collect dust. Anyway, I just…I just keep trying."

His lips quivered slightly at his own admission.

Pilar jumped in. "Well, we think you're kinda special and we wanted to take your mind off it and give you a little break."

"Ladies, I appreciate it, and I'm happy to take a break with you. Thank you for being so thoughtful and bringing me a beer."

The women beamed.

"But—" Maury paused as he took a long sip of his beer. "I'm afraid you don't really understand. You see, this agonizing over words, plot points, phraseology, and all the other things that go into telling a good story is, well, it's delicious agony. I love every minute of it.

"You see, I truly look forward to struggling, to trying to find not just the right word, but the *perfect* word. A single word so worthy that it paints a beautiful picture in the readers' minds. A word so perfect that it erases all ambiguity and helps the reader understand some new truth that changes everything.

"I may look like I'm unhappy, but I'm far from it. I treasure every scuffle I have as I flesh out the story and take it from an obscure idea in my head to a completed work that I can share with others. So, you see, things are not always what they seem. And I—"

Maury stopped talking, and his eyes took on a faraway look. He hurriedly glanced at his manuscript and, in a low whisper, verbalized what he was thinking. "Of course! Things are not always what they seem to be. I know what my character can do now. Oh, man, it was so obvious."

Suddenly, he looked at the two women as if surprised that they were sitting there. Picking up his pen, he said, "Please excuse me. I have to rewrite this section right now before I forget my thought."

He didn't wait for an answer. He started writing immediately, and it was clear to the women that they should return to their seats at the bar.

Amused, they glanced at him now and then as he alternately smiled and grimaced, writing furiously. Pilar leaned toward Theresa and whispered, "Ballard! It takes all kinds."

# MEMORIES

Samuel Amundsen was eighty-three years old, but at 6:30 A.M. he rose from his bed as usual, showered, read the sports section of the morning paper, and had a full breakfast served to him by eight o'clock. His wife, Sigrid, who was five years younger, got up a half hour after him and cooked that breakfast, serving him the moment he sat down at the kitchen table with his copy of the *Seattle Times*.

Shoveling in the last remnants of his egg and hash browns, Sam said, "You know, you do pretty good work around here."

"Just pretty good? Are you sure?" she asked.

"I may have understated it. I don't want you getting a big head about it," Sam replied.

"OK, just for that, I have to tell you that the pay for this job is way too low, nonexistent, in fact, and I'm thinking of resigning," Sigrid said.

Chuckling now, Sam said, "You think I can't cook up my own breakfast?"

"I know you can't. Where's a pen? I'll be giving you formal notice," Sigrid countered.

They both chuckled quietly. Sixty years of marriage resulted in the same scene being played out multiple times.

Sam finished his meal and stated what he always said after the meal. "Don't go throwing away the paper. I have to read the front and Northwest section later. Not enough time now."

"Taking your walk?" Sigrid asked, already knowing the answer.

"You betcha. I'll be back when my feet get tired."

Sigrid checked the clock. "OK, it's eight forty, so I'll be looking for you around eight forty-five or maybe eight forty-six."

Sam kissed her on the cheek and said, "Oh, you old people—always getting tired so fast. I'm still young, so I may be gone till midnight. Don't wait up for me."

Sigrid smiled. She'd heard all his jokes before.

Sam took the elevator down to the main floor of the Merrill Gardens and stopped at the front desk to check the daily bulletin and shoot the breeze for a few minutes with the attractive young ladies at the desk. As the hallway clock struck nine, he headed out the front door on 56th Street and turned left.

Immediately, Sam heard the voice he expected.

"You're late," Mel Finch said flatly.

"Am not. You always say that. You're so predictable," Sam countered.

"Jeez, he starts in right away with the insults. Couldn't you just be nice first for a while," Mel said.

"What's the fun in that? Which way you wanna go today?"

Mel hesitated and followed with a barb. "You're mighty feisty today. I think you should pick. That way you can't criticize me if we go a direction you don't like."

Sam nodded and said, "I'm feeling nostalgic today. Let's walk up Market and complain about everything that's changed."

Mel smiled his agreement.

They walked east on Market until they came to Ballard Avenue. Turning right, they walked down the street, commenting on every new restaurant or bar. When they got to the 5300 block, Mel said what he always said. "My gramps used to work right here at the JC Penneys. It was a big deal back then to have a Penneys in Ballard."

"You've told me this story a thousand times," Sam said.

"Yeah, and I'll tell it to you a thousand more if you last that long. It's a good story about how he got promoted, got transferred downtown, and worked there for thirty years. You just don't have any real appreciation for history, do ya?"

"You always say that too," Sam replied.

"I have a theory about why you don't care about history as much as I do," Mel stated.

Purposely, Sam didn't bite. He just kept walking.

"Don't you want to hear it? My theory, I mean," Mel said, pleading just a bit.

"Not really," Sam said, trying to appear as uninterested as a teenager at a paint drying contest.

"Good, I'm glad you asked. See, my theory is that your brain is just too small. You aren't really even close to as smart as I am."

"OK, now let me tell you some—"

"Oh, hey, look!" Mel said, interrupting. "Here's the place from that picture I showed you. Yup, 5233 Ballard Ave. Gramps used to go drinking and pool playing at the bar that was here. Long gone now."

"Fascinating!" Sam said. "Is that another historical gem for my benefit?"

"You bet. No charge for that one," Mel said, laughing.

"Let's go up to twentieth and head toward Market. I'll show you some history," Sam said.

"You wouldn't know history if it rose up and smacked you in the face," Mel replied.

They walked side by side up twentieth, stopping briefly, as usual to look in the window of the Monster, Art and Clothing store. Sam stared at the pictures and odd items they displayed there.

"Go ahead, say it," Mel urged.

"I love this place. It's just cool," Sam said.

"You say that every time. I mean, I like it too, but do you ever ask me what I like about it? No."

Sam laughed. "Your feelings are hurt so easily. Come on, I promised to show you some real history."

They walked up to Market and looked west, gazing at the one of the oldest buildings in Ballard.

"Now that's history," Sam said as he pointed unnecessarily. "The old Carnegie Library. And this tiny brain knows when it was built and when it closed down. What do you think of that?"

They stopped across the street from the building and admired it.

"They don't build 'em like that anymore. That is one fine building. OK, smartypants, when was it built?"

Sam breathed the fresh morning air, enjoying the moment. The salty air was so strong, they could have been standing on Shilshole Beach. "Started construction in 1904, finishing and opening the library in 1906."

Mel considered that and asked, "Do you know the exact day? Or the time of day they started building?"

Perturbed, Sam said, "No. Do you?"

Mel laughed. "Haven't got a clue. But I remember when they shut this place down—1963. Not a good year for a lot of reasons."

"Dodgers liked it," Sam said.

"There you go with the baseball trivia again. See, I'm more of the intellectual type. I don't spend my time memorizing who won the World Series or what Willie Mays hit that year."

Sam nodded. "C'mon, let's go up the corner here and see if you can tell me what used to be here."

"Ooh, a test. I'm excited now," Mel said, acting unimpressed by the whole thing.

They walked to 15th and Market and stood on the northwest corner. "What was here back in the day?" Sam asked.

"Too easy. Hell, way too easy. You and I came here together lots of times. Denny's! The Taj Mahal of Ballard, that's what people called it. Remember that?" Mel asked.

"I remember everything. Where'd it all go, Mel?" Sam asked. His voice broke just a bit.

Mel didn't answer. They walked up 15th all the way to 62nd, then hung a left. As they were walking to the next stop, Mel said, "We forgot to go look again at Fire Station 18."

"Oh, darn. I love that building. Ever go in the side door and go all the way up to the top of the tower?"

"Yeah, quite a few times. Used to walk Astrid up there all the time. She goes regularly to see the doc at Divine Spine. They got a nice place up there. Astrid liked all the folks there. I mean, she still does," Mel said, a bit wistfully.

"That firehouse—that's a fine building," Sam said. "And speaking of fine buildings, here's another." At 1763 NW 62nd, the Interfaith Community Sanctuary stood, just as it has since 1890.

They both admired it for a few minutes. Sam broke the silence, saying, "See, I have a deep appreciation for good architecture, and I have a theory of why you don't. Wanna hear it?"

"Not really," Mel said. "I think I know it already. Does it have something to do with how small my brain is?"

"Bingo! Give the man a Kewpie doll!" Sam exclaimed in his best announcer voice.

"Careful, you're dating yourself. People will know you're really old now. Nobody these days knows what a Kewpie doll is."

"Hell, even *I* barely know!" Sam said, laughing. "I just remember my dad always saying that."

"We better head back to the barn. My feet hurt," Mel said.

"You old people. You're such softies."

Mel nodded. They both smiled as they walked the last few blocks toward home.

As they got to the door, out of the blue, Sam said, "Dodgers won the series, sweeping four games from the Yanks, and Willie hit .314 with 38 homeruns."

Mel nodded as though he expected it. "And you're telling me why? Trying to bore me with trivia?"

"On the contrary. I tell you for two reasons. The first one is that I'm trying to help you and your tiny brain expand a bit and embrace new thoughts."

Mel considered that and looked at his friend sideways. "And the second reason?"

Sam laughed. "Who else am I going to tell?"

"Ain't that the truth. Same time tomorrow?" Mel asked.

"Lord willing, I'll be here," Sam said, sniffing and wiping at his nose.

Mel nodded and disappeared around the corner.

Sam entered the lobby and silently slipped past the front desk. He took the elevator to the fourth floor and put his key in the door. Entering, he saw his wife picking up a hot dish with two oven gloves on and heading for the door.

"Now that's what I call timing!" she said.

"Where are you going?" he asked.

"Up to see Astrid. She's still listless. Two weeks now and she just can't let go of Mel. I'm just going to go spend a little time with her."

A somber Sam nodded. "She misses him a lot."

His wife looked at her husband of sixty years and knew what he was thinking. "I know you do too. I'll be back soon."

He closed the door behind her and thought to himself, *Yup, I miss my best buddy, but when I go for a walk, it's like I can still hear him. I think he'll always be with me.*

# THE LAST PLACE

Will Hardesty walked down 17th and turned right on 57th Street, heading for the Common's Park at 22nd. It was a warm summer day, and he wanted to relax and catch some rays at the park. He had his Jack Reacher book with him and was looking forward to getting deeper into it.

Arriving at the park, he took a seat on an empty bench facing the water fountains that the kids ran through. He made sure to position himself so he didn't get too close and end up as wet as the kids. Settling in, he opened his book and started reading. Every few minutes, he'd look up to see what was going on and do a little people watching. His reading pace wasn't setting any world records, but he didn't care. This afternoon was just for relaxing.

He read for a while longer, then looked all around, trying hard to soak in his moment in the afternoon sun. His mind wandered, and he started thinking about his wife, Christine, and wondering if she had given up on him. He was into his eleventh week of unemployment, but as hard as he tried, he found no work for an x-ray technician. There were some jobs in Tacoma and one other one in Marysville, but for a man without a car, the commute simply didn't work. He realized he may have to take any job just to bring some money in. He knew Christine wasn't happy. Finances were incredibly tight even when he had a job, but this latest spell, brought on by the hospitals' merger, was breaking them. For a second, he thought about how he couldn't afford a gift for her birthday next month. And he thought about his disappointment with his own birthday a few days ago.

He shook his head quickly, trying to dispel those negative thoughts. As he did, out of the corner of his eye, through the seat slats, he spied something purple lying under the bench. Reaching under it, he took hold of it and brought it up into view. It was a knitting of some kind, all purple and what looked like a gold *V* nearly finished on one end of the item.

Considering it, he realized someone must have dropped it there by mistake. He rose from his seat, got down on all fours, and looked around under the bench, seeing exactly what he expected—a silver knitting needle. Searching further, he determined that the other member of the needle pair was nowhere to be found.

He smiled to himself and thought, *Cool. A mystery. Someone was working on making, well, making something. A sweater, maybe, or a scarf or something. Knitting right here on the bench and she—OK, it could've been a he, but I doubt it—she stopped her work and pushed it into a purse or bag, but it fell out, and later she would look and not have any idea where it could have been lost. She might be looking for it now. Well, this gives me something to do. I love sleuthing novels; now I have a mystery of my own to unravel.* He chuckled at his own apropos choice of words.

*I'll unravel it all right. And I know just where I'll start.*

Will walked over to JOANN Fabrics and Crafts store, directly across the street from the park. Spotting an employee stacking some items on the shelves, he strode up to her to ask for help, but another customer beat him to it and he stopped to look around for someone else. *Popular place*, he thought to himself. Seeing everyone very busy, he started strolling the aisles, searching for purple wool. He found multiple shades of purple on aisle A-36.

Realizing how unlikely it was that any salesperson would remember a customer who bought this shade of purple weeks or a month ago, he turned around and headed for the exit. *C'mon, Will. Think! This is Seattle, the home of the*

*UW Huskies. Purple is a favorite color here. It could be anybody who bought it.*

He stopped suddenly in his tracks and thought, *Of course. But what about the knitting needle here? Maybe this would lead me—*

He stopped in midthought when his eyes landed on a shelf holding dozens of identical needles. Many were silver, others gold.

*Great, the needle is as generic as it gets.*

Embarrassed, Will looked around and, not wanting to make himself look like a bigger fool, exited the store. He stuffed the item into his jacket pocket and headed home.

A week later he wore the same jacket, and as he put his hand into his pocket, he immediately realized what he was feeling. Suddenly, a new idea hit him. He took a picture of the item and used his computer to create a flyer showing the lost knitting and needle and printed out ten copies. He stated where it was found and put his cell number on the flyer.

Checking the time and seeing he had ninety minutes before Christine would get home from work, he quickly set out on his errands. He posted the notice on a bulletin board in JOANN, then went to the Venue on 54th and 22nd and posted another. Thinking hard of where else artists or craft fans go, he went to the Dakota Art Store at 20th and Market and posted another.

Finally, he returned to the park and posted the rest on telephone poles nearby. Satisfied he'd done all he could, he returned home and started working on fixing dinner.

Christine arrived home at six o'clock and saw her husband in the process of making dinner. Things had been a bit strained between them lately, and as much as she didn't mean to be, she was a bit curt. "I hope you're not fixing Top Ramen Surprise again," she said.

"No, I was just making some chicken soup with, you know, some extra vegetables and stuff in it. I made a salad too," Will said. Noticing the look on her face, he asked, "Not a good day for you?"

She shot him a look. "There are no good days, you know that. I hate this job. Did you go out looking for work today?"

"X-ray technician jobs aren't really something you look for, Chris. I cleaned up here and tried to stay busy."

Trying hard not to take out her bad day on Will, she asked, "Did you use the Starbucks card I gave you yet?"

"You mean the one for my birthday? Yeah, I did. Doesn't take very long to use up ten dollars."

"Jeez," Christine exclaimed. "That's not fair. I'm working every day. I couldn't really even afford that."

Will shook his head. "I know you're mad at me, Chris, but what am I supposed to do? So I don't have a job right now. Is that it? You don't love me anymore? You used to give me wonderful presents. Things you really poured yourself into. What do I get this year? A debit card."

"Well, it's probably more than I'm going to get. I think you need to go accept any job you can. Amazon is hiring. So are a lot of other companies. The economy is still hot. Can't you just swallow your pride and take any job?" She collapsed on a chair and buried her head in her hands.

Will tried to focus on the dinner preparations. Neither one of them said anything for a few minutes. Finally, Christine came over to her husband and put her arms around him. "I'm sorry, Will. I *do* love you. I always will. I'm sorry about your birthday. I was making something for you. A scarf. I was almost done, then I must have dropped it on the street or some—"

Will's eyebrows rose and his eyes widened. He looked at his wife and said, "Oh my God!" Then he started laughing. He hustled over to the foyer closet.

Christine, taken aback at his demeanor, backed away. "I wasn't trying to be funny. What are you doing?" she asked.

Will returned to her and held out his hand. "Was this what you were working on?" He showed her the purple knitting.

It was Christine's turn to appear stunned. "How…where did you—"

"I found it under a bench at the Common's Park."

Christine started to laugh but caught herself. "Wait a minute. Why do you have it here? Why would you pick it up?"

"I thought it was kinda cool. You know, Husky colors, and I saw the V on it, and I thought, 'Oh man, some guy named Vance, Victor, or Vinnie didn't get his present.' So I tried to find the woman by playing detective and leaving flyers and stuff. All along…all along—"

"It's always in the last place you look!" she said, cutting him off.

"Yeah, but what's with the *v*?"

"It's not a *v*, silly. It's the first half of a *w*. A *w* for Will. The guy I love."

Will picked her up off her feet and kissed her. "Yeah, and it was you I was looking for all along. Story of my life, babe! Story of my life."

# THE SPREE

His mom and stepfather were arguing again. He couldn't sleep anyway, so thirteen-year-old Grady carefully eased his bedroom door open and crawled out onto the landing at the top of the stairs. Still staying out of view from his parents, he listened in on their conversation.

"It's not all his fault. It's a new school for him, and the year just started. He keeps finding himself in awkward situations on the playfield. And I'm not sure that teacher, Mrs. Hobart, really likes him all that much," Grady's mother said.

Grady could almost hear his stepfather shaking his head.

"I know you believe that, but I say he's an accident waiting to happen. You say he finds himself in those situations. I say he causes them himself. He's always been a handful. Hell, he comes home with blood on his shirt all the time. He's been fighting. He's smart enough, but he doesn't apply himself. Honestly, Brenda, he'll never amount to anything."

"Don't say that. Clay, I remember you saying that you got into lots of trouble yourself when you were young," Brenda asserted.

"Not as much as him. He won't ever be anything good. I expect he'll find himself in prison before he's eighteen."

Grady could hear his mom pushing her chair out and standing up. If it had been Clay getting up, he would have made a lot more noise, plus he always grunted a bit when he stood up straight.

"I don't want to talk about it anymore," Brenda said. "I'm going to bed."

Quickly, Grady slipped back into his room, closed his door as silently as he could, and moved directly into bed. He knew his mom would peek in to see if he was asleep. She always did that on her way to their bedroom. He pulled the covers up and slowed his breathing.

The door opened, and his mother looked in. She sent a silent prayer his way and went off to bed. Grady listened as she closed her door, and he knew the other noise he heard was Clay opening the refrigerator for another beer.

Grady lay in bed rethinking all he heard. It wasn't new. He'd heard it all before.

The bell at Monroe Junior High School rang, and the seventh-grade classroom emptied in a flash. Another scholastic day had ended, and Grady picked up his books and left the room, nearly last as usual. As he emerged into the sunlight, he saw Rick Stuart and Howie Morgan leaning against the fence. As soon as they saw him, they motioned for him to come over.

Howie was the largest of the three. Three years ago, he heard of a college football player who was nicknamed Badger. He really liked that name, so he insisted that the kids call him the Badger. Now everyone called him that, even the teachers.

"The Gradster! How you doing?" the Badger asked. Not waiting for an answer, he said, "I got us some plans for the weekend. Something that will get everybody talking. Maybe even be on the news. You want in on it?"

Grady blinked twice as he tried to think fast. Too late.

"Of course he does, Badge," Rick said, smirking at Grady.

"Good, 'cuz it's gonna take three of us. We need a lookout, and that's you, Grady."

"Guys," Grady began, "I...I'm not sure—"

"Shut up, Grady. Just do as you're told. You want another beating?" Grady was slight-of-build, a mixed-race teen who had lately become the Badger's favorite punching bag.

The Badger sneered at the smaller boy and flexed his muscles.

Grady gave a shake of his head. "What am I looking out for?"

Rick rolled his eyes. "Jeepers! You really that dumb? Cops and stuff, you idiot." He turned to the Badger and asked, "What's the plan?"

Looking rather smug and pleased with himself, the Badger replied, "Not now. Not here. You two meet me by the empty liquor store on Market, you know, the one near the Taco Time. Be there at eight o'clock. I got some special shopping to do between now and then, and that's when I'll show you what I got."

Excited, Rick nodded, slapped the Badger on the back, and grinned.

Shaking his head, Grady suggested, "Guys, why don't we just go over to Grumpy's Comics on Market and see what they've got that's new?"

Badger stared at him and said, "You're boring, Grady. We're meeting at eight. Be there."

Grady nodded his reluctant agreement and headed home to 59th street, near 30th. He took 20th Avenue to Market Street and headed west. As he passed 24th, he spotted a gray-bearded man struggling with some heavy boxes and shelving units out on the sidewalk. Sensing an opportunity to make some spending money, he crossed to the south side of Market and stepped up his pace.

John Watkins, the owner of Twice Sold Tales, grunted as he moved some large boxes full of books onto a hand truck.

"You lookin' for some extra help, mister?" Grady asked.

"I wasn't," John said. "But my back is killing me and it sounds pretty good right now. I'll pay you ten bucks if you help me move all the books in and onto the shelfs and then help me move these old shelving units to the back."

"I can do that. How about fifteen?"

"How about nine?" John countered.

Grady smiled, realizing he knew which way this negotiation was going to go. "Twelve seems like a good number."

Laughing a bit, John agreed, "Twelve it is!" He introduced himself and shook the boy's hand, then showed him what to do.

For the next forty minutes, Grady moved everything inside, stacking the books on the lower shelves as John instructed and moving the shelving units to the back of the building where he stored his extra items. When they were finished, John said, "You did good, boy. You've got a good work ethic."

Grady said nothing. He just smiled.

John doled out twelve dollars into the young man's hand. Grady stuffed the bills into his jeans pocket. "Thanks, Mr. Watkins. I can use it. It was lucky I came across you when I did."

"Son, you are luckier than you know. I'm an old man, but you've got your whole life ahead of you. I'm telling you, you can do anything you set your mind to if you really apply yourself. So listen to me—fact is it's all up here." He tapped his head with his index finger twice. "Work hard and get as much schooling as you can. You'll do well. You'll make something of yourself. You might even own your own business someday, and you know what the best thing about that is?"

"I'd get rich?" Grady asked.

"No—well, maybe you would, but that isn't the point," John said. "When you own your own business, you have the freedom to build your life as you want. You can make your own decisions and figure out how *you* want to live. It isn't all about money. It's about choices."

Grady looked down at his shoes and mumbled, "Not too many people think much of me."

"Look at me, Grady," John ordered.

Grady raised his eyes to meet the shop owner's.

Staring firmly back at him, John said, "Grady, were you listening? It's not about what others think. It's about what *you* think. But for what it's worth, I believe in you. I think you've got what it takes."

Grady nodded, mumbled his thanks again, and left, the twelve dollars firmly in his pocket.

After dinner, Grady slipped out when no one was looking and met up with Rick and the Badger by the old abandoned liquor store. The Badger was standing there holding a bag with something heavy in it. After talking for a bit and building up the suspense, he said, "Boys, we three are going on a spree tonight. Lookee at what I got!"

He opened the bag and showed them six bottles of spray paint: two red, two black, and two green.

"Here's my plan," Badger began. "We meet again here at two thirty. The bars will be closed and the drunks on their way home. The street will be deserted. We're gonna paint our tags on every business up and down Market Street from here to Twenty-fourth. We'll hit them all. Rick and I'll use red and green while Grady warns us if traffic or people are coming. Grady can use the black to just spray anywhere except on our tags. You don't even have your own tag, do you, Grady?"

"Um, no, but, man, if we get caught, there'll be hell to pay."

"You chicken?" Rick asked.

"I just don't think it's such a hot—"

"Shut up," Badger barked. Back in command mode, the Badger said, "Now, we all go home and go to bed. Set your alarm and we'll meet right here again at two thirty, got it?"

Thinking fast, Grady said, "What are you going to do with the paint? You can't let your folks see it."

Clearly the Badger hadn't thought that part through. "Oh, yeah, good thinking, Grady. Might be hope for you yet. Maybe I could hide it in our garage and—"

"No way," Grady said, interrupting him. "Your dad might find it and then you're screwed. I got a better idea. These trees lining the back of the parking lot are perfect. See how the branches hang way low? Just put the bag well back behind one of the trees, and we'll come back here tonight and get it. No one will see it back there."

Rick and the Badger exchanged a glance and smiled. "He's right."

The Badger went to the third tree from the left and crawled close, placing the bag behind it, out of view. "See you guys at two thirty. Set your cell phone alarms."

Rick and the Badger headed east toward their homes. Grady walked the other way toward 32nd. Every few minutes, he would look back to see where the other two were. When he saw them nearing 24th, he turned around and went back, retrieved the bag, and carried it home. He went around to the basement door and slipped inside, leaving it unlocked. He placed the bag under a load of junk in the basement that hadn't been moved in years.

Grady showed up at the dumpsters at two thirty-five, hoping the other boys beat him there. They had. And they were standing around with long faces.

"Is something wrong, guys?"

"Yeah, something stinks. The bag is gone," Badger said, just a bit too loud.

"Gone? How could that be? Who would steal that?" Grady asked, trying hard not to overplay it.

"This sucks! It was such a good plan," Rick whined.

"So I got up for nothin'? You two guys wasted my time. We could've had a spree and now we got bupkus. I'm outa here. And you know what, don't call on me again. You guys are losers."

Feeling deflated by the evening's events, the Badger momentarily forgot that he was the leader and he should beat some sense into Grady for what he said. Instead, he hung his head and cursed his bad luck.

Grady walked home, slipped into the house by the back way, and snuck up the stairs to his bedroom. Clay's snores drowned out whatever noise he might have made. He climbed into bed and covered up.

Alone in the dark, he smiled and thought to himself, *John said he believed in me. He said I could make something of myself. I sure as hell wasn't gonna let those two idiots deface his store or any others. This is the new Grady, and it doesn't matter now if no one else believes in me. I believe in me and that's enough. I'm gonna work hard, 'cuz now I know what I want to do. I want to own my own business, just like John, right here in Ballard. And someday, I'll be somebody.*

# FINAL SCORE

Reggie walked through the front door and immediately made eye contact with his girlfriend. "Final score was seven to four; Mariners won!" he called out triumphantly.

Layla nodded unenthusiastically and walked into the bedroom.

The next morning, Reggie woke her up at six fifteen and was gone out the front door before she could get out of bed.

Layla was thirty-six, a seventh-year nurse at Swedish Hospital in Ballard, and could easily walk to work from their apartment on 57th and 20th. Reggie was a longshoreman who most often worked an early shift at Pier 91. They dated for a year before she left her apartment and moved in with Reggie.

That morning she dressed in a crisp and clean uniform, as usual, and headed into work. Halfway through the day, she was dragging.

Marsha, a coworker, noticed her slower pace and caught up with Layla as she finished her rounds. "You feeling OK?"

"Yeah, sure, fine. Why?" Layla replied.

"Well, you kinda look like you're, I don't know, uninspired or something."

Layla shook her head as she prepared to deny it again, but her lips betrayed her and she blurted out, "This whole thing with Reggie is looking like a big mistake."

"The moving in thing?" Marsha asked.

"Yeah. It's all different now. We used to do things together—you know, go to dinner, take walks, catch a movie. Now he goes to work early, so I don't see him in the morning, and nearly every night he goes out to the bars and watches the ball game with his friends. We're hardly ever alone together unless we're asleep. It's just not working for me."

"I assume you shared this with him?"

"I started to a few times, but he's always in a hurry in the morning or on his way out the door to the bar every time I get home," Layla lamented. "It's like…like he's avoiding me."

Marsha said nothing. She understood human nature well, and she knew her job today was only to listen.

Layla looked at her friend and knew what she had to say next. "I'm going to confront him tonight. I can't keep doing this."

Marsha nodded and said, "Do it, girl. Let me know how it goes."

Arriving home at six thirty, Layla came in to a dark apartment. Once again, Reggie wasn't home, and if he had been, he left all the lights off. She hated that. She flipped the wall switch and illuminated the room. Walking in farther, she saw a note on the dining room table. *Off to catch the M's game. See you around 10:30. R.*

Pressing her eyes closed silently, she committed to herself that she would stay up and force the issue tonight.

At 10:52, Reggie put the key in the lock and opened the door. He stumbled in and, seeing Layla staring at him from the couch, said, "Final score, Angels thirteen, M's two. Terrible game. I think I had too much to drink."

He walked past her to the bedroom and removed his shirt and pants and collapsed on the bed.

Giving in to the inevitable, Layla went to sleep on the couch and woke the next morning when Reggie mumbled something to her and closed the front door behind him.

"How'd it go?" Marsha asked the moment Layla reported for her shift.

"It didn't. He was drunk. He walked into the bedroom and passed out on the bed."

Marsha shook her head. "I'm sorry, Layla. You don't deserve that."

"I don't. He comes in every night and immediately announces the score of the game he was watching with his buddies. Like I care. I mean, I actually do enjoy watching some sports now and then, especially when we're talking together about the game and other things. That can be fun, but he never asks me to go with him and he treats me like live-in help. You still got room on your couch for me if I need it?"

"You bet, but I hope it doesn't come to that."

Layla scraped a tear off her cheek and said, "I'm not sure it can come to anything else."

She worked her shift and headed home, certain that she knew what she had to do.

She arrived home to another note. Same message. She pulled out her suitcase and began packing.

At ten fifteen, Reggie arrived home. "Final score, Sounders three, Portland two! What a great game. Really enjoyed it tonight." His smile evaporated as he viewed the luggage on the floor. "What's this?" he asked.

"I got another final score for you. Layla one, Reggie nothing. I'm out of here, Reg. I give up."

"What do you mean? What's wrong?" Reggie asked.

"You don't even know, do you?" Layla said, shaking her head. "Before I moved in here, you would take me places. We'd go out to dinner, movies, or the museum or whatever, and we'd talk and do something fun. Now that I live here with you, you go out by yourself practically every

65

night to Market Arms, or Fitzgerald's, or Olaf's, or somewhere to be with your bar friends. So I say, if you prefer them to me, then you go hang out with them all the time, but I'm leaving."

"Wait! You don't understand," Reggie protested.

"Enlighten me, then!"

"Oh, jeez, Layla, I'm sorry. I used to go to the bars a lot to have a drink and watch part of the game, but I did it so I could have someone to talk to. You know, other guys."

"So with me gone, you'll get what you want, right?" Layla asked.

"No. Oh, hell, Layla, I don't have any real friends. Those guys are all young professionals. They don't want to talk to an old longshoreman. I just hang out and watch the game. Before you moved in, I could watch and do whatever I wanted. For example, I used to like my Wednesday ritual where I'd broil some dogs and eat beans and wieners for dinner. I didn't have to look my best or nothing, and the remote was mine. I'd just surf all night until I found something that kept my attention. When I suggested we get a TV for the bedroom, you said you didn't want it, so I couldn't surf anymore. I felt like it wasn't even my home since you came in, and I guess I was kinda mad."

"That's your apology? That's not even a good excuse for the way you've treated me."

Reggie sat down in the chair opposite the couch. "I'm sorry. I love you. I don't want you to go."

"So what are you saying?" Layla asked. "Are you saying that putting a TV in the bedroom so you can surf and eating hot dogs and beans solves all these problem?"

"No. Yes. I don't know. Maybe it's a good start. I haven't lived with anyone since I moved out of my mom and dad's house. I don't really know how to do it. Tell me what you want me to do and I'll change."

"Reg, I'm not asking for anything special. OK, I'm not a big fan of hot dogs and beans, but if you want to eat those on Wednesday nights, I can fix a big salad or something. If you wanna surf, I'm OK with a TV in the bedroom. I just want to feel like your best friend again. And I want us to talk like we used to. I like baseball. Football I might like if I understood the deal with all the hankies and stuff, so maybe you could teach me. I'll go watch a game with you now and then, but you and I have to have some together time too."

Reggie stood up and tentatively moved closer to her. His muscular arms reached out, and she rose and allowed herself to be engulfed by them.

As he hugged her, he whispered in her ear, "I'm sorry. I totally screwed this up. Give me another try."

"I will. I want this to work too," Layla said.

"There is one thing—well, two things, though," Reggie said.

"What?" Layla asked, not sure she really wanted to know.

"First Seahawk preseason game is tomorrow night. Want to go to Fitzgerald's with me?"

Laughing, Layla replied, "OK. You said two things. What's the other?"

Grinning widely, Reggie said, "They don't call them hankies. They're flags, OK?"

Laughing again, Layla said, "OK. Final score Reggie one, Layla one. We're going to overtime."

# A SPECIAL KIND OF LUCK

My name is Paul. Earl is my buddy. I met him seven years ago and we got along well. Now we hang out together nearly all the time. Earl isn't much of a talker, but I'm OK with that. I don't speak much myself.

When Earl and I hang out, we visit some of the bars in Ballard and have a drink. Sometimes two or three. Often, we go down to the Market Arms and join the crowd. We both like everything about being with a crowd, feeling the excitement that watching a ball game at the pub generates and cheering along with everyone else.

Earl works at the Gates Foundation, designing some kind of manuals for distribution in third world countries. He tells me about it sometimes, but I don't really understand it. He likes his work, and I'm sure he wouldn't know what to do with his time if he didn't have it, so that's a good thing.

But I feel bad for Earl. He's gone through some hard times in his life, had a bad accident, and has morphed into some kind of loner—not in the usual sense of that word, but he just is. He doesn't have many friends besides me, and I know he wishes he did. He used to have a girlfriend, someone he was serious about, but it didn't work out. I get it. I'm sort of in the same boat.

Right after we met we started to go on long walks around Ballard together. We'd get some fresh air and enjoy each other's company. He'd say, "Paul, let's walk to the locks today." Or he'd say, "Let's go see Leif," and we'd walk down to Shilshole and stop at the statue of Leif Erickson, pat the base for good luck, and head back. Why Earl thought patting the base would bring good luck was beyond me, but he did. I didn't mind; I'm easy going and not much bothers me.

Now, seven years later, it was spring again. The air smelled fresher, the sun was brighter, and we enjoyed our walks a lot more. We spent a lot more time catching the Mariner games. He likes baseball. I can take it or leave it, but I can tell it makes him happy. He likes the history of the game, and when the announcers say something about Felix or Cano breaking another record, he always comments on it.

But beyond those few highlights, he's lonely. I know he'd like to meet a woman his age to talk to and connect with. I'm, like, no help in that department. I can't do anything for him there. It's not like I know a ton of people either. I just work and do my job, and I don't meet anyone who I can introduce him to or anything.

We were sitting around one day on the porch, a warm day in June. He was nursing a drink of some kind. I had finished mine. All of a sudden, he stood up as though a bolt of inspiration hit him. "Paul, I got me a wild idea. Let's walk across the Ballard Bridge and go down to Fishermen's Terminal where all the boats are docked. That'd be different. I like smelling the sea air and the salt water up close. It's a cool place, but I haven't been there for quite a while."

Since neither of us has a car, and since we don't really need one in Ballard, with its high walking score and all, we hoof it everywhere. He was right; it would be good to see something different. We headed out, walked up 59th to 15th Avenue and then south toward the bridge. Traffic gets a bit dicey there for walkers, but we got onto the pedestrian path and walked across. Cars would fly past in their lanes, causing a vibration I could feel up and down my spine. I knew Earl felt it too, and I could see he was smiling and having a good time. Earl is easy going like me. He appreciates the simple things in life.

When we arrived at the Terminal, we walked toward the piers, in front of the open doors of Little Chinooks, where the aromas of fine cooking wafted past our noses. Earl said, "Mmm, smell that? Fish and chips. I love that smell. Let's get some before we leave. I've had them here before. You'll like them."

I was salivating already, just thinking about it.

We headed down a random pier and stepped carefully around equipment, hoses and spare parts lying in our way like an obstacle course.

As we did, a woman, about thirty-five I'd say, moved from a boat up onto the pier. She looked at us and said, "Out for a stroll?"

I'm awkward around women I don't know, so Earl spoke for both of us as usual. "It's such a great day. We just wanted to get out and enjoy the fresh sea air and maybe steal a boat and go on a thrill ride."

The woman laughed. "Whoops. You just told me your secret plan."

Earl laughed. I just smiled. She was nice. Healthy, long hair, a vibrant smile, and I liked her eyes.

"Well, now we'll have to do it another day," Earl said, still smiling.

"Hi, I'm Denise," the woman said and held out her hand. I nudged Earl. He's so clueless sometimes.

Earl extended his hand and shook hers. "I'm Earl," he replied. "This is my pal, Paul."

I shook her hand too and smiled. I was glad Earl was doing all the talking.

"I'm very glad to meet you. Would you care to come on board and pretend you're a sailor?"

Earl gladly took her up on it, but I held back. I didn't want to get in his way in case he wanted to put some kind of move on the babe, so I relaxed on the pier.

After some time, Earl returned and we headed back to get some fish and chips.

The woman emerged from the boat again and called out to us. "Earl, um, you know I showed you my kitchen. I can cook on this boat too. Would you care to come by tomorrow afternoon and have lunch with me?"

Earl looked distressed. I could tell he was nervous, but I'll give him credit, he recovered well. "That...that'd be great. What time?"

"Twelve thirty or so? I'm a good cook. Paul is welcome too, of course."

"OK, cool. We'll be there. Thanks. See you then."

We turned and walked back to Little Chinooks. Earl was chuckling to himself. "It's weird, Paul. I just had this feeling we should go to Fishermen's Terminal today. I felt like something cool was going to happen and it did. I got a date. I got a date!"

Earl went inside and placed an order while I waited in the shade. We sat down at an outdoor table, and Earl took a bite of the cod before breaking off a piece for me. I scarfed it down.

He reached down and patted my head. "Wow, now that was a special kind of luck today. Blind luck, huh?" he said, laughing. Then he looked down at me, smiled, and said, "Good boy. Think you can lead me here again tomorrow?"

I barked affirmatively. I knew I could. It was my job.

## סטארבק תרגום

Jon caught Linda's eye and nodded toward check stand four. Linda rolled her eyes. She wasn't serving anyone, so she left her stand and idled over to Jon's stand number two.

"I don't get it. Neither of us have anyone in line, and she has a customer she's serving and two more standing there waiting their turn," Linda whispered.

"I know. And if Larry were watching right now, he'd be expecting us to go over and offer to help check the others in line so they don't have to wait," John whispered back.

"Pointless. Been down that humiliating road already. I hate it when you offer and they look at you like you're bothering them. They never change lanes once they're in hers." Linda headed back to her post, seeing little point in having this conversation over and over again as they always did.

At check stand four, Rachel Cooperman was forcing a smile at her current customer and handing change to her as their transaction completed.

Next in line was a dour-faced man in his seventies. He had but two items, a can of whole cranberries and a bag of chili seasoning.

Rachel ran them through the scanner and said, "Congratulations, you win today's award for the most unusual combination of purchases."

Expressionless, the man stared back at her.

Not getting the smile she was hoping for but undeterred, Rachel said, "It looks like these two together would be an interesting meal. Sure you don't need anything else?"

He shook his head, apparently uninterested in prolonging the conversation.

"Do you have a discount card I can scan?" Rachel asked.

The man pulled out his car keys and displayed the mini-card attached to the ring.

Rachel took it from his hand, examined it, scanned it, examined it again, and said, "This little card is in remarkably good shape. I'm going to take a picture of it and nominate it for finest card of the month." She smiled a quirky little smile at him.

For a brief second, the man's mouth twitched as though it were about to erupt into a smile, but then he returned to his customary frown.

Not giving up on her mission, Rachel followed with another line. "In fact, I like this card so much, I really want it for my very own. How much will you take for this card? How about five hundred dollars?"

"How about six hundred?" the man deadpanned.

"Oh, great! Sold!" she said, beaming at him. "Your car goes with it, right?"

Shaking his head, as if this had been a contest and he had lost by a whisker, the old man finally smiled and replied, "No car for you. I never let anybody else drive my car."

Rachel laughed and handed back the keys as she said, "Have a good day, sir. Come again."

The next customer stepped up. She was a regular and greeted Rachel like a long-lost friend.

Jon and Linda just shook their heads.

Rachel finished her shift, picked up the notebook she had under the shelf, and headed home to Ballard. She was renting a small apartment in the basement of a home on 22nd near NW 64th. She didn't stop anywhere or dilly-dally on the way. When she returned home, she opened up her notebook and checked her work. Talking to herself, she said, "Got three more today, Raelyn. Two youngsters and the old man." She wiped a tear from her eye and went straight to her makeshift studio.

There she selected three blank three-by-five canvasses, her paints, and a brush. From memory, she painted them all with a serious countenance, just as she had done with all the others. She painted the face of the young boy she had convinced to smile early that morning by feigning shock that he was already five years old. Then she portrayed the twelve-year-old girl who had come in so unhappily with her father. Commenting on her choice of low-cost makeup, she told her how she had made a wise choice and the shade she picked would look really good on her. Finally, she captured the serious look of the old man. She pinned all three to the wall along with the others from this month.

After eating, showering, and reading her book for a short time, Rachel set her alarm for work and prepared for bed. Seconds before she turned out the light, the phone rang.

"Hello, dear," her mother said.

"Hi, Mom. What's up?"

"Something has to be up? A mother can't just call her daughter to say hi?"

Rachel gave her a chuckle, certain that was what she was after. "Thanks for calling, Mom. How are you?"

"I had a very busy day. They keep us old folk busy here at the home. One road trip after another. Went downtown to Nordstrom today. Bought a new scarf. How about you?"

Rachel swallowed hard. "Just worked today. Nothing special."

An awkward silence followed. Rachel pressed her eyes closed, knowing what question her mother would ask next.

Finally, in a voice a few decibels lower than before, she asked, "How many now?"

Trying hard not to just hang up, Rachel wiped her eyes and gave her the information she knew she craved. "Nine hundred seventy-eight."

Without any other response, he mother said, "Good night, dear."

Rachel shut off the light and climbed into bed. As she tried to drift off to sleep, her mind returned to that night in Shoreline. Almost three years ago. She and Raelyn were celebrating being twenty-one. It was their second night out in a row, visiting bars and loving their new life as legal drinkers.

Rachel lifted her head off the pillow and shook it violently, trying hard to not replay it in her mind again. It didn't matter. She knew she would. It was her penance and she had no choice.

Raelyn returned to their table with two more beers and two young men in tow. They sat together and laughed through two more rounds. At eleven thirty, the strapping fellows said they had to go and invited Rachel and Raelyn to ride with them to another bar. Raelyn made eye contact with her twin sister and gave a subtle negative shake of her head. Rachel dismissed it and said, "Cool! We'd love to go with you." Still protesting, Raelyn climbed into the front seat with the one named Drew as Rachel took the back with Seth. Fifteen minutes later, what was left of the car was wrapped around a telephone pole. Drew and Raelyn lay dead on the ground. Seth had a head injury. Rachel was virtually untouched.

After finishing the scene in her mind's eye, she pushed herself deeper into her pillow and went to sleep. As Rachel finally drifted off, she could still hear Rabbi Mendlowitz saying, "Rachel, I know you don't believe me, but it wasn't your fault. You can't go on through life like this. Your mother, bless her heart, can't bear to see you like this. She says you have no hope left in you. This thing, this mountain of guilt, is blocking you. It's so wide, you can't get past it. It's so tall, it blocks out all the light. It's so thick, no hope can penetrate it. I'm telling you, there is only one way for you to live with this." Speaking partly in Hebrew, he said, "It's called סטארבק תרגום."

The next week was routine for Rachel. She worked her Tuesday through Saturday shift at the grocery store and continued to do her best to follow the Rabbi's advice.

Feeling an urge to speed up the סטארבק תרגום process, on Saturday afternoon after her shift she stopped in and perused the children's book section at the Secret Garden Book Shop on Market. Christy, the store owner, saw her struggling with choices and approached her. "Can I help you find anything?"

"There are so many books to pick from," Rachel replied.

"I can help with that. What are you looking for specifically?" Christy asked.

Shaking her head, Rachel said, "I'm not sure exactly. I'm trying to find about eight or ten short, low-cost books with general appeal for kids, you know, maybe six and under."

As Christy thought for a moment, Rachel quickly added, "I don't know the kids. I…well, I work at the store on fifteenth and now and then I see young children coming through my check stand who are unhappy or crying, and I wanted to have something fun I could give them. Kind of maybe in this price range." She pointed to one book she had already picked out.

Immediately, Christy said, "I know exactly what you need. And, by the way, I think it's really nice of you to do that." She walked over to another shelf and started pulling smaller books and handing them to Rachel. When she had passed her eight books, she said, "All of these are priced like the one you showed me. And they're all cute stories. The kids will love them."

Rachel thanked her and made her purchase. The following week she began handing them out when the opportunity arrived. They didn't fail her. She added more and more paintings to her wall.

Late one Friday afternoon, with the November wind howling, she finished her shift and started the walk home. She decided to go a different way and walked down Market Street, watching all the young people enjoying an evening on the town. Tempted to stop at the Pie Bar as she passed, she knew she had a meal already left over in the fridge, waiting for her. *Pie is for dessert. Maybe I'll come down here later or maybe tomorrow and get some of that bumble berry crumble.*

As she walked, she remembered back to that day in Temple. The Rabbi told her about סטארבק תרגום, and she stared back incredulously at him. "You think that will do it?"

He locked eyes with her, gave her that penetrating look that made her believe he knew every dark thought she had ever had, and said, "You spend too much time feeling the hurt inside. You need to stop thinking about yourself and start feeling other's pain. It's all around you. Don't think about you. Think about them. Find those that are hurting inside, and even if it's for only one moment in time, make them smile."

"Rabbi, I know you care, but I don't think finding one person out there and giving them a brief moment to smile is going to change anything about what I did."

The Rabbi smiled back at her. "Oh, Rachel, you're right. No simple task can take your hurt away. Nothing ever will. You miss your sister too much. You will *always* feel the hurt. What I'm telling you to do won't take the hurt away, but it will poke some holes in that giant roadblock in your way, and over time, you will see some faint slivers of the light of hope peeking through. Right now, you have no hope at all. I'm just saying this is a way to get some back."

"One at a time?" Rachel asked, tears streaming from both eyes.

"One at a time," the Rabbi said. "Do a thousand. Keep count. And when you're done, let me know if anything's changed."

"A thousand? That'll take me years."

The Rabbi looked at her calmly and whispered, "It'll take years anyway."

Rachel turned on 24th and headed north. As she passed 62nd Street, a woman wrapped in a blanket sat on the ground, leaning against a telephone pole, shivering in the early evening cold.

Rachel passed her by, stopped walking, and turned back. Bending over so that her head was almost even with the woman, she said, "Are you all right, ma'am?"

"I got nowhere to go," she mumbled. "I spent the last of my money on breakfast yesterday. I thought…I thought I might just give up, you know, right here."

Rachel reached into her purse and pulled out a twenty-dollar bill. "Here, take this. Get some food."

The woman frowned and shook her head. "I'll just be in the same situation tomorrow. I got nothing. What's the point?"

Realizing cash was not going to help, Rachel put her hands on the woman's shoulders and helped her stand up. "C'mon, you come with me. I live real close. I've got food at home. I'm not the very best cook, but I can make something for us both that you'll like."

Smiling for the first time since Rachel spied her, the woman mumbled her thanks, and Rachel helped her walk steadily the remaining three blocks to her apartment.

After cooking up some hot soup and sharing last night's leftovers with her, the woman lay down on the couch and fell asleep.

Rachel watched her for a while, then sat down at her work desk. She pulled her notebook out of her purse and looked over her list. She hadn't painted in three days, yet she firmly remembered every one of the seven people she had described in her notebook. She began painting deep into the night. When she finished the last of them, she counted the pictures on the wall, added them to the count she had at the end of October, and let out a low whistle.

"Nine hundred ninety-nine," she whispered to herself.

The old woman stirred. Turning over to face the back of the couch, she covered herself up again. Rachel watched her and suddenly realized that the woman had smiled when she invited her to her home.

*Number one thousand,* she thought.

Rachel immediately took out another empty canvas and painted the old woman's face. Unlike all the others, she felt compelled to show her smiling. She pinned the picture to the wall and stood back to admire her work.

Again the old woman stirred. She woke and sat up. Clearing her eyes, she strained to see her host and the wall of pictures. Finding the strength to stand up, she walked over next to Rachel and pointed to the last picture on the wall.

"Who are all these people?"

Rachel hesitated, then said, "Just people I've met here in Ballard."

"Is that me?"

Smiling a genuine smile, not a forced one, Rachel replied, "It is. Do you like it?"

The woman moved closer to it and examined it again. "I'm smiling. It shows me smiling. You took me in and gave me food. You got me out of the cold."

"I didn't do much," Rachel said.

"Yes, you did," the woman disagreed. "You gave me something I haven't had in a long time."

Not totally sure what she meant, Rachel asked, "What's that?"

"Dearie, you gave me hope. Maybe there's a chance for me yet."

Swallowing hard, Rachel nodded. In a whisper, she said, "Of course there is. There's a chance, and a little bit of hope for all of us."

They both stood in the middle of the room staring at the wall of pictures. Her memory of Rabbi Mendlowitz returned and she could hear him saying, "One at a time. To a thousand. The only way is with סטארבק תרגום."

Under her breath, she repeated it to herself, "תרגום סטארבק. The Long Good-bye."

# LIKE MINDS

Margaret and Heidi met every Thursday at one of the many upper-class restaurants in the Ballard area to enjoy a wonderful dinner. This Thursday in September was no exception. They were nearly the first ones there when the restaurant opened at four. A few other tables were occupied, including one in the corner behind them where the guests were apparently in the powder room.

Seated at their favorite table on the south side of the room, the two sixtysomething women had an unobstructed view of the front door so they could see everyone coming and going. This was also their favorite table because they knew that Ethan Blaine, the smoothest waiter in Ballard, worked that station and attended to their every need.

As they took their seats, Ethan came by quickly as they were still settling in. "I so look forward to your visits, ladies. Serving you truly makes my day. What can I do for you today?"

Margaret went first and ordered the gem lettuce Caesar salad; Heidi selected the spinach salad with gorgonzola. For the entrée, Margaret opted for the grilled scallops while Heidi followed with an order for the roasted duck breast. After he noted those items, he looked back at them expectantly. "Would the ladies enjoy a fine bottle of wine to share tonight?"

Margaret and Heidi both chuckled. "Ethan, you're so precious. You know we always order our entrées and let you select the perfect bottle for us."

"I never assume, ladies. But, if you wish I have in mind a bottle of superior sauvignon blanc that would complement those meals so well, your taste buds will rally together in tumultuous revolt and sue you if you don't have another."

Heidi put her napkin to her mouth to stifle her laughter. Margaret didn't care who heard her laugh.

When Ethan departed, the two women settled down to work. The real reason they were there. Both of them had been raised in Ballard and had made it their business to know everyone else's business. Residents of the area were known by both or at least one of them. Seconds later, the front door opened and two more customers were escorted to a booth.

Heidi looked at Margaret and they both nodded at the same time. "Every night at the same time, just like us. Right on time too. I don't think they ever eat at home. Jeffrey Harper and Elise. They aren't happy you know," Margaret said.

Heidi nodded. "Who doesn't know? He went to Vegas for business, and she hasn't been happy since."

"Ooh, look. Bill Brewer at the front door and who is that? His cousin?" Margaret asked.

"No, that's interesting," Heidi replied. "It's Martin Slater. He owns the barbecue place in Freelard. I wonder if Bill is going to invest some of that money he made when he sold Microsoft short a few years ago."

"I was wondering what he would do with that cash. Oh, look, it's—"

"Ladies!" Ethan interrupted. "Your salad is served. Here's a plate for each of you and I brought you each a rose. Nothing special, just something I like to do once an hour or so for the most beautiful women in the building."

Heidi and Margaret cooed their pleasure, instantly agreeing with Ethan on his decision to reward them with the honor.

He served the salad and said, "I'll be right back with your wine."

Back to work again, Heidi pointed at the door. "The whole brood again. Jim Westbrook, his wife and three daughters and two boyfriends. That tall one—he works at Amazon but I can't remember his name."

"David Mays," Margaret answered. "He's a little too smarmy for my tastes."

"You thinking he might ask you out soon?" Heidi said, stifling a smile. Margaret laughed and said, "Probably not. He's too young to understand the magical allure of older women."

"Too true," Heidi agreed.

Ethan returned with their wine. Carefully pouring a small amount into each glass, he said, "I think both of you need to test this and approve it, or not. Whatever you say."

They both swished their glasses around, made a big show of enjoying the aroma, then took a sip so small little birdies would have been envious.

"It's perfect, Ethan, as always," Margaret said. Heidi smiled and nodded her agreement.

The moment he left, they were back to work. "Look who's leaving already," Heidi said, pointing to the door.

Margaret made her tsk-tsk noise. "As usual, she only sits at the bar. That was less than thirty minutes for Matty. She usually stays a bit longer. What do you think?"

"I think she's been unhappy for a long time. Maybe she's finally getting over it. Gotta admire her; she never overdoes it. No one has to prop her up or wheel her out as she leaves. That woman is a disciplined drinker. Where do you bet she's going now?"

"She likes to top off the martinis with a margarita. I'd say El Borracho or the Matador," Margaret said. "Whatever she's going through must be really tough."

After a few quiet moments, Heidi said, "They say her man left her. She didn't used to drink that much."

"My man left me fifteen years ago. Of course, I hate to say it, but that turned to out to be a good thing," Margaret replied, shaking her head and chuckling to herself.

As Heidi struggled to think of a smooth segue to change the topic, Ethan appeared at their table again.

"Ladies, your entrées are here." He placed them on the table and said, "I had a personal question for both of you if you don't mind."

Margaret's and Heidi's faces lit up as they relished the idea of a "personal" question.

Ethan seemed to pause, as though he were afraid to ask. With the drama raised to the peak that he desired, he asked, "Does it take you a long time?"

The women exchanged a glance. Margaret said, "Does *what* take us a long time?"

"Well, to get ready, of course. I mean, dressing up and putting the perfect amount of makeup on, and all the other preparations you must make to show up here looking so stunningly beautiful that Helen of Troy herself would be jealous."

Both women closed their eyes and leaned their heads back, enjoying the moment.

Heidi broke the silence. "Ethan, it takes no time at all for us. We just roll out of bed looking perfect."

Margaret gave a subtle nod as though it were all true.

"Ladies, I believe you. That doesn't surprise me at all. True beauty needs no assistance." His eyes twinkled as he flashed a knowing smile at them.

As he left, both ladies downed half their glass of wine and tried to recover. Then it was back to work.

A woman entered the restaurant alone.

"That's Katy St. John," Heidi said. "Works at the Inn. I always thought that was a made up name. I mean, really, sounds like Hollywood to me."

"It sounds phony to me, too. Maybe she's on the run from the law and decided to go out in glory with a hot name."

"Oh, this gets better," Margaret added. "I think she's meeting someone. Bet he's married."

"And there he is!" Heide said as a tall, dapper young man came in the door. "I hate it when they're outsiders. I don't know him. Any ideas?"

Margaret shook her head. "No. How frustrating. Not a clue. You know what that means."

"Married, meeting on the sly. Bet he works downtown. I mean, we can't know everyone!"

They both looked at each other and smiled wickedly, conjuring up all sorts of salacious thoughts.

A busboy came by and took their finished entrée plates. Seconds later, Ethan showed up with two orders of cherry cobbler with vanilla ice cream.

"I didn't want you lovely ladies to have to wait. I know how you love your deserts."

For just a moment, they each imagined Ethan was sending them a secret personal message in the way that he stated that. Neither said anything, but both would have gladly taken the young man home for desert any day.

"He likes us a lot," Margaret said, watching Ethan walk back to the kitchen.

"I think we make his day for him. He enjoys serving women who understand this world and make it a brighter place."

As they completed their meal, they both looked at each other and smiled. "We know, don't we?" Heidi asked, already knowing the answer.

Margaret nodded. "We know everyone and all their secrets. And we know human nature, and that's why we're always certain we're right about people—even when we aren't."

Heidi smiled widely, in full agreement. They paid their bill, leaving a twenty-five-percent tip for Ethan, and headed to the front door.

In the corner table behind them sat two women in their seventies, Abigail and Maureen.

"There they go." Maureen said. "I guess they're finished making all their comments about everybody as they're coming and going."

"Those two think they're always right, just like we used to," Abigail said.

Maureen smiled back at her friend. Chuckling a bit, she added, "Yeah, we're older, so now we must be right, right?"

Ethan showed up at their table with their entrées. "Ladies, as usual, you have ordered the very best dishes in the house. How you divine what is best every night is beyond me. Your intellect is exceeded only by your rare beauty."

"Oh, Ethan. You devil," Maureen said, laughing.

"He's a pretty sweet devil, I think," Abigail added.

Ethan left their table after flashing a quick flirtatious smile.

Maureen glanced at her friend. "We know, don't we?"

Abigail nodded. "He likes us. Why? Because he appreciates class."

"I thought it was because he was paid to like us," Maureen said, smirking.

"Well, yeah, there's that. I just enjoy imagining that he *really* does like us. Let's not ruin the moment."

A couple entered the front door. Abigail started in first. "Ooh, someone new. We better find out all about them." The two of them got back to work.

# THE EXPERIMENT

In a single-story house on NW 63rd Street and 17th Avenue, ten-year-old Mikey Hausman had his eyes glued to the TV screen when his mother entered the family room holding his coat.

Her name was Claire, and she announced, "C'mon, Mikey. We're going for a walk."

"No! I wanna watch this."

"You can see that anytime. And besides, you're supposed to be upstairs doing your homework," his mother said.

His dad entered the room. Barking just a bit, he ordered, "Shut it off, Mikey. We're walking down to the locks to get some exercise. And at three o'clock, one of the biggest yachts in the world is coming in from Russia, and I want to see it up close. You can too."

"Cool!" Mike replied, suddenly interested.

"He's supposed to be doing his homework, Michael," his mother said, shooting a glance at her husband.

"What homework do you have to do, Mikey?" his father asked.

"Mr. Jefferson says we have to design an experiment of some kind and test it out."

"Like what?"

"Like, well, anything. I mean, we have to form a...a...hypa—"

"Hypothesis?" his father asked.

"Yeah, that thing. You know, how we think it will turn out, and then we have to do it to see if we were right."

"So what are you going to do?" Claire asked.

Rolling his eyes, Mikey said, "That's what I'm supposed to figure out."

His father shook his head and said, "When we get back, no TV. You think about it during our walk down there and back and then finish your homework assignment."

Mikey said nothing. He knew he was running out of time. His report was due tomorrow.


A half mile away, at quarter to four in the afternoon, in an apartment on 24th Avenue and NW 64th, Else Fain turned down the covers and padded the pillows on the bed, lining them up perfectly. She hung her clothes up in the closet and dusted the tops of the desk of drawers. She looked around at her humble surroundings and gave herself a satisfied nod. Everything was in its proper place.

She picked up the picture of her late husband on the dresser and held it in front of her. Speaking out loud, knowing full well no one could hear, she said, "Daniel, it's been a long sixteen years since you left me. My family has all passed, and my best friend is in a home with Alzheimer's and she no longer remembers me. Today is my eightieth birthday. Not one card. Not one call. I'm invisible. No one knows me and no one cares. Why I'm still here, I have no idea. What purpose do I serve? All I want now is to be with you. So today…" She choked on the words and stopped talking. She wiped at her eyes and finished her sentence. "Today I'm coming to you."

She put on her gray coat and selected one of her three canes, the one that Daniel had bought her just before he passed.

Else headed outside for her last walk. She left the building and turned south toward Market Street. As she took her first few steps, she heard a bird tweet, and suddenly she remembered something her mother had told her seventy-two years ago when Else's grandmother died, surrounded by family and friends. Her mother made note of the gentle smile that was pasted on her face as she died, and she said to Else, "See, girl, she died happy and content. When you die happy, it's as if you never died at all. The ones you loved most in the world are there to greet you, take you by the hand, and lead you on up to heaven."

Else digested that thought, as much as an eight-year-old could, and asked, "What happens if you don't die happy?"

Her mother looked at her as if that thought had never occurred to her, stammered, then replied, "Well, I guess you can still go to heaven, but you have to go alone, and when you get there, I think you have to find your loved ones yourself." Seeing that answer didn't seem to satisfy her young daughter, she quickly blew it off and admitted she was just guessing. She didn't really know.

Her mother never imagined Else would remember that conversation for the rest of her life.


At three fifteen, Mikey, Clair, and Michael Hausman all exited the park by the locks and headed east on Market Street, back toward home.

"Can we stop in at Seven Eleven and get some ice cream?" Mikey asked.

"Not this time, Mikey," Claire said.

"That was some yacht, huh?" Michael asked.

"It was so cool. I bet it cost a million dollars," his son said.

"I think the newspaper said it was a *lot* more than that. No danger of us ever buying one, I can guarantee you," his father responded.

They walked a little farther, and Mikey stopped to watch a climber carefully working her way up the Climbing Gym, the rocky cliff face outside Stone Gardens. "Mom, look at that. We should do that sometime. They rig it up so you're super safe and everything. Wanna do it right now?" he asked, hopefully.

"You've got homework, young man. Nice try. But it does look fun, so maybe someday," she answered.

After walking up another few blocks, Mikey stopped to look in the window at the Portal. "Oh man, I want to do this. Can we, Mom? Dad? Sometime?"

"What is it?" Claire asked.

"It's VR, Mom," Mikey answered simply.

"Same question. What's VR?"

"Virtual reality," Mikey said, amazed that his mother was so clueless. "You put on headsets and you can go into a different reality and fight monsters or walk a plank a mile high or whatever.

It's really cool. Some of the guys at school have done it, and they say it's super cool."

Michael glanced at his wife with an amused expression on his face. "Well, that cinches it, then. If the fifth grade at Salmon Bay says it's cool, then it's definitely cool. It might be fun. Tell you what, you do your homework and get a good grade on Mr. Jefferson's experiment assignment, and I'll bring you here for a test run, OK?"

"OK!" Mikey replied. "I'm gonna really think about it now and come up with something good."


Else passed by the QFC and continued on her walk toward Market Street. Planning now, she thought to herself, *I'll get to the busy intersection at the northeast corner and wait in front of Kitchen and Things. I'll stand underneath the overhang and pretend to be looking in the window at the store. I'll just wait a few minutes, and when the timing is right and the Metro 44 comes flying by, I'll just take a little step off the curb. It'll be fast. I don't have to worry about anyone stopping me. I'm invisible.*

The Hausmans waited for a break in the traffic, then crossed Market Street at 26th Avenue to get onto the north side of the street. As they walked, they passed an older couple who were strolling slowly in the opposite direction. They weren't talking, and Mikey thought they didn't look very happy either. He continued to think about his project, growing a bit desperate as he felt time slipping away.

With the sunlight already growing a bit dimmer on this early October day, Else spotted the Metro 44 heading down Market. It appeared to be stopped before Ballard Avenue. *I'm not afraid. I wish…I wish I were happy, so…* She stopped thinking, not wanting to finish the thought. She swallowed hard and moved just west of the load/unload zone at the curb. *I'm invisible. No one will stop me.*

As they passed the old-style gas station and stopped at the northwest corner of the intersection, little Mikey pulled on his mother's coat and said, "I got it!"

"Got what?" his mother asked.

"I know what I'm going to do for my experiment. In fact, I can start right away!"

As her son finished his proclamation, the walk light came on and she put her hand on his shoulder, propelling him forward. The three of them crossed the street as the light was changing again. The westbound traffic was moving swiftly on Market as Mikey left his parent's side and hustled forward.

The thought *I wish I were happy* flashed through Else's mind as she saw the 44 picking up speed approaching the intersection. She swallowed hard again, still trying to time it right, as she prepared to take the step off the curb. At the moment her brain sent the signal to take the step, an open hand was thrust in front of her. Startled, she saw a young boy smiling at her and heard him say, "Hi. I'm Mikey Hausman. What's your name?"

The bus passed as Else tried hard to pull herself back into reality, away from the darkness that her mind had gone to.

"Um, what?" she asked.

"I said I'm Mikey Hausman. What's your name?"

For the first time today, Else broke into a smile. "Well, Mikey, I'm glad to meet you. My name is Else Fain." She spoke the words, astonished at what she was saying.

When the young boy just stood there smiling, she asked, "How old are you?"

Mikey's face erupted into an even larger smile. "I'm ten, but I'll be eleven in just three months!"

"Oh, my! Very good. I'm eighty years old. And *today* is my birthday."

"Wow! That's old. Well, happy birthday!" Mikey said.

By this time, Claire and Michael had caught up with their son and were standing beside him as a few bystanders glanced their way before continuing on their own travels.

Claire leaned over toward the diminutive woman in the gray coat and said, "I hope my son isn't being a pest. I don't know what got into him, but happy birthday to you."

Else smiled back and said, "Thank you. It means something to me to hear you say that."

Claire looked at her son, trying to fathom what he had done and why. Sensing it was getting awkward, she said, "Well, we have to be going. I hope you have a wonderful birthday day."

They said their good-byes, and Mikey gave a good-bye wave.

Else stood there, frozen in place, watching the small family move along up the street. Ten seconds later, she realized she was still smiling.

"What in the world was that all about, Mikey?" his father asked.

"I figured it out!" he said proudly. "I saw lots of old people walking around and they weren't smiling, so I decided to try an experiment. Instead of just passing the old people by, I decided I'd step up and introduce myself and say hi and maybe then they'd smile. And, you know, maybe just meeting them would make something good happen, like making them smile and be happy. That was my—my, you know, hyparthenon."

"Hypothesis," his dad corrected, laughing.

"Well, it certainly seemed to work on Else, but that was only one test. Don't you have to do more?" his mother asked.

"Yup! And look, how about that guy? He looks kinda old and grumpy."

Before they could answer, Mikey had quickened his pace and made a beeline for the old man ahead of him.

Claire and Michael held back to watch their newly inspired son conduct his test on the streets of Ballard.

Else felt reenergized. She felt full of life, and suddenly she had a revelation. *What have I been doing to meet people and get out more? Nothing. I stay home and then wonder why I have no friends, why I don't run into anyone I know or feel a part of things anymore. This is on me. I can change that. I've spent so much time feeling sorry for myself because everyone I know is gone that I forgot there's a whole world full of young people and some of them may want to talk to me!*

She continued walking up Market, determined to go to the Coffee Works, order a latte, and relax as she continued to work on the plan forming in her head. She thought about all the elementary schools in the area and how she might be able to help. *Maybe I can tutor. That would be fun. I know my numbers, and I was always good in English. I could help some kids and meet some people.*

She was full of thoughts racing through her head, and the more she thought about it, the wider she smiled. She crossed the street fully enveloped in this new hope she had found. *On Monday, I'll go up to the Salmon Bay school and—*

Else never noticed she was crossing against the light. She never saw the pickup truck come flying through the intersection.

A few moments later, she opened her eyes and there was Daniel. Her mother stood beside him. They smiled brightly and both extended their hands to help her get up.

# THIRD GRADE WISDOM

Third grade was brutal. At least, in Katie Emery's mind it was. Her teacher, Mrs. Palmquist, seemed to be on fire today, spouting off about a dozen new ideas one after another. She was talking to the class about volunteering and helping out in the community. At one point, she listed off example after example of what individual class members could do as Katie tried desperately to keep up with her, jotting down as many as she could remember.

Exhausted from her mental gymnastics at the end of the day, Katie walked directly home to her house on 63rd near 30th NW. She collapsed in a chair and lamented to her mom. "Now I gotta do more work. Mrs. Palmquist wants us to do some kind of volunteer job. It's not fair. I already have too much homework. Second grade was easier. I don't like this."

Sagely, her mother nodded and pretended to agree with her. She brought her daughter a cookie and said, "Tell me about your day. What did Mrs. Palmquist suggest you do?"

Katie reeled off some of the things she remembered, and she pulled out a handout that the teacher had sent home. Still complaining, Katie said, "I was trying to write stuff down as she talked, but she was going super-fast, and then she gives us this paper, and see, everything she said was all written out on it. I didn't have to write it myself after all. How was I supposed to know that? Third grade is really hard!"

Again, her mother nodded in faux agreement and looked over the list. "What do you think you'd like to do, Katie?"

"I don't know."

"Oh, here's a nice one. You could pick from one of these names of retirees and write a letter to them once a week. That would be fun," her mother suggested.

"Mom! What's fun about that? More work. Just more work," Katie protested.

Hiding her amusement, her mother replied, "I thought you liked to write. You can just make it short and tell them about how school is going, or what you watched on TV, or what games you played. People like to get that kind of mail."

"That's fun?"

"It can be, Katie. You should try."

Shaking her head, Katie said, "I'll do something else. Something more fun." She grabbed the list of things to do and started reading through them.

"All right. I just thought you might think it was fun to get something in the mail."

Katie stopped reading. "What did you say?" she asked her mom.

"Well, let's see here," her mom said, feigning forgetfulness. "Oh, I remember. I said it might be fun to get something in the mail."

Katie thought about that for a moment, then turned her head at an angle and asked "What would *I* get?"

Enjoying the moment, her mom replied, "Well, you'd get letters back, of course. If you send a letter to someone, they usually send something back to you."

Katie's eyes went wide. "I'd get some mail?"

"I bet you'd get a lot," her mother said and watched as her daughter's face lit up, sealing the deal.

Katie glanced again at the handout and saw a list of names of retirees living at Merrill Gardens. She smiled, pointed to the list, and said, "How about this one? His name is George, just like Grandpa."

Before her mother could respond, the newly energized Katie rose to her feet and raced to her room for a pad and pencil. Returning to the dining room, she sat at the table and began to write. "Dear George," she said, then glanced at her mom. "Is that OK?"

"I think he'd like that," her mom said.

She wrote furiously without help from her mother, telling George all about herself, her friends, and her school life. When she was done, she had filled six pages and proudly showed her mom. "Can we mail it right away?"

"No. But *you* can mail it right away. It's not raining. Take it up to the mailbox on 32nd and then come right home." He mom finished addressing the envelope and placed a stamp on it. Katie took it from her hand and raced out the front door to mail her treasure.

Three days later, Katie arrived home to find mail had arrived for her.

"My first mail!" she exclaimed, leaving little doubt that the reward had been worth the effort.

She sent another the next day and got George's response asking her to color a picture of her family for him. She dutifully fulfilled his wish and sent it off.

Katie and George exchanged letters for three straight months, and Katie never seemed to tire of it. On a cold day in February, she mailed a letter containing more drawings, but no response came back.

After a week, she wrote another letter, asking him if he liked the picture she had drawn. There was no response.

For the next five weeks, Katie stuck to her assignment, sending off one letter, usually on Wednesdays, but George never responded.

In mid-March, she gave up. "He must not like me anymore," Katie told her mom.

"Well, honey, he's probably very old. Maybe he had the flu or just doesn't feel well. Did you ever ask him that in your letters?"

The young girl shook her head. "No, he usually asked the questions. I just answer them or try to draw the picture he wants to see. Now it's all ruined. This isn't fun anymore. I don't like it."

Her mother grew more solemn as she contemplated some worst case scenarios. Finally, she made a different suggestion to her daughter. "Honey, how about you and I go together down to Merrill Gardens?"

The decision made, they agreed to wait no longer. They left their house ten minutes later, driving to the senior living home.

Upon their arrival, Lisa Palm, the operations director, was summoned, and she escorted Katie and her mother to her office. Seated, Lisa did her best to break the news to Katie. "Honey, George was very old. He had no relatives around, and getting your letters was something he greatly looked forward to every week. But, honey, his heart was bad, and it gave out a few weeks ago." She paused to make sure the young girl understood.

"He died?" Katie asked.

"Yes. He had a full life, and you made his last months much more fun for him. You should be proud of that," Lisa said.

Katie sat at the edge of her seat, trying to show a brave face. Her lower lip quivered as she whispered, "I don't even know what he looked like."

"You come with me. We've got pictures of everyone here, and his is still up on the board."

Lisa walked her two guests down the hall and stopped at a poster board full of pictures. "This is from last Christmas. And right here"—she pointed to a slight man with thin graying hair, smiling back at the camera—"is George, sitting by the tree."

Katie smiled back at him. "He looks friendly," she said.

"He was," Lisa assured her. "And he had a wonderful laugh."

Sensing they had done all they could, Katie's mom took her hand, nodded to Lisa, thanking her with her eyes, and led her daughter back toward the exit.

"Wait, Katie! I almost forgot," Lisa called out. She hurried to her office and removed a file from a cabinet. Opening it up, she pulled out a single piece of paper from George's file and handed it to Katie.

The young girl looked up at her and waited for a clue what to do.

"We found this in his room. He hadn't finished. It's for you," Lisa said.

Katie opened the letter up and read it aloud. "'Dear Katie. I loved your picture of the Ballard sunset you drew for me. Thank you very much. I wish I had a granddaughter just like you. Maybe someday you can stop by and visit me in person.'"

Katie looked at her mother. "He didn't sign it. It's not done."

Her mother wiped her eyes and patted her daughter's head. "I think it's perfect just the way it is, honey."

They headed, once again, to the exit. Katie held George's last letter tightly in her hand. As they passed the front desk, they noticed a large gathering of older men and women in the lobby. A woman from behind the desk announced, "Mail is finally here. Everyone ready?"

Several voices called back to her. One man laughed and said, "What do you think we're waiting here for?" Many laughed.

The woman took the top letter and said, "Mary Turner!" A cheery woman stepped forward and took the mail from her hand. "Big Ben!" she called out, and a tall man stepped forward to claim his prize. Katie and her mother were transfixed, watching the seemingly routine event becoming a highlight of the day.

Lisa eased up beside them as the last few names were called out. Those who received a letter seemed to scurry off to somewhere private to read their treasure. The room cleared out, but one lonely woman remained, sitting by herself in an armchair. For just a second, the woman locked eyes with young Katie, and she nodded to the young girl.

Katie turned to Lisa and said, "She didn't get any mail, did she?"

Lisa shook her head. "Tilly usually doesn't. I don't think her family is much on writing."

Katie wiped a lone tear from her eye, and once again, they said their good-byes to Lisa.

When they got back into the car, Katie said, "I wish I coulda met George. He looked nice."

Her mother just nodded.

They drove home in silence. As they pulled into the driveway, Katie said, "I'm going to write to Tilly. Then she could get some mail too."

Her mother stared back at her and said, "I think that would be real nice. I'll call and find out her last name, OK?" Then, as an afterthought, she said, "You sure like getting mail too, don't you?"

"It's OK. Even if I don't get any from her, I'll still send her stuff. After seeing them all, you know, I sorta get it now."

Her mother, unsure of her meaning, studied her facial expression. "Get what, Katie?"

"You know, it's not about *me*, is it? It's about them."

Her mother leaned over and hugged her. Half laughing, half crying, she said, "You're pretty smart for a third grader!"

# THE IDEAL PLACE

Sarah Ahlberg left her job at the end of her shift at the Nordic Museum. She worked the admissions desk for her first eight months, but moved up to be an assistant to the Collections Coordinator a few months ago. It had been the ideal job for her, and every day she found herself in a good mood when she arrived at work and when she left. *Find a job you love and you never have to work a day in your life,* she thought to herself as she exited, thirty minutes after the museum closed at five o'clock. Her apartment was only a few blocks away, a stone's throw from the Ballard Locks. *My commute is only about five minutes on foot! Can't beat that!* She smiled, amused at herself for thinking that same thought every night as she left work.

It was good that she had a job she loved because the rest of her life was in shambles. Alex, her boyfriend of six years and her roommate of the last four, had packed up one day last month and left her a note saying he didn't want to settle down. He was gone, and she hadn't heard from him since then. Lately, they had been fighting more. She kept suggesting they should talk about making their relationship more permanent, and he would act interested but was never willing to take any steps to make it happen. Now, even though she had the job of her dreams, she was struggling financially, as the rent on the small studio unit had become a significant portion of her take-home pay.

But tonight was Friday, a beautiful summer night, and Sarah didn't want to dwell on negatives. She stopped in at the Lockspot and walked straight into the bar. Kristen bartended on Fridays, and they had gotten to know each other a bit. As she sat down, a glass of sauvignon blanc materialized in front of her.

"Sarah! Give me some good news," an ebullient Kristen said, smiling her biggest smile.

Thinking fast, Sarah countered, "I have wine!"

"Too obvious," Kristen said, laughing. "Any other good news?"

"Tell you what. Give me some time to down a few sips and maybe I'll think of some."

Kristen shot her a look that said, "I know, you're still hurting." She didn't have to say anything else. Another customer signaled for a refill and she turned her attention to him.

Sarah sipped her wine and tried not to turn the event into another pity party. *I've done that too often already.*

"This seat taken?" a voice to her left asked.

Turning, she confronted Wade Ibsen, an accountant at the museum. They knew each other and had exchanged some chit chat on occasion.

"Wade! Hi. Sit down. Let's get Kristen to—" She stopped midsentence. Staring at his half empty schooner, she continued, "Well, no need to order a drink for you."

"I was sitting over there"—he pointed to the left—"watching the Husky game. They're shooting well tonight and have a big lead, so I thought I'd join you for a moment if that's OK. I mean, unless you were expecting somebody."

"No, I just stopped on the walk home for one drink." *Better stick to that now, Sar. Don't want Wade thinking I'm a big boozer.*

"I know, I like this place too. I usually come in on Friday nights to celebrate getting through another week without, you know, transposing any digits or accidently leaving the decimal off a two-hundred-dollar check," Wade said, chuckling a bit to make sure she knew it was a joke.

They talked for another twenty minutes until both their drinks were empty. As Wade downed his last swallow, he said, "Gotta get going. Got a sixty minute drive to Mukilteo. I really envy you for living so close. I'd love to find some place I could afford around here."

"What are you looking for?"

Wade rocked his head back and forth a bit and said, "Well, something in my price range. I've got student loans to pay off, so that makes it a challenge. You know, maybe a one-bedroom for twelve or fourteen hundred a month."

Sarah's eyes widened. "Yikes! That's what I pay for a studio. You're going to have to look really, really hard."

Wade laughed. "Yeah, I know."


A week later, Sarah found herself watching the clock and looking forward to exiting after five. She headed down to the Lockspot and spotted Kristen behind the bar. Using eye contact to telepathically submit her usual drink order, she took a seat at the bar and looked around the room.

"He's not here yet," Kristen said.

"Um, a, what? *Who's* not here?" Sarah said as Kristen rolled her eyes. They both started laughing, and Sarah said, "Jeez! That obvious?"

"You two hit it off last Friday. Sometimes I think we should call it the Luckyspot."

Sarah shook her head and said, "I don't really believe in luck." She accepted her white wine and looked around again. No Wade anywhere to be seen.

She pressed her eyes closed and berated herself for her silly romantic notion. Sealing her thoughts, a heavyset man, more her father's age, took the stool left of her, hemming her in between him and a pair of women on the right. She took another sip, committed now to finishing fast and exiting with some modest amount of grace left.

It was then that she felt a tap on her shoulder. She turned to see Wade smiling back at her. "Wow, look at this place. It's packed. Must be giving the fish and chips away for free tonight."

Clumsily, Sarah stuttered, "Um, hi. Hi, Wade."

Wade looked her over and said, "I almost didn't recognize you. Your hair's different, and this is a really nice suit you're wearing."

"Oh, thanks, you know, bad hair day and I salvaged what I could." *He noticed. Alex never commented on any new hairstyle or anything new I wore.*

"Well, hey, I'm hungry, so I'm going to have a dinner here in the restaurant. Care to join me?"

Agreeing in record speed, she joined Wade, and they enjoyed a fine dinner and each other's company during a slow, relaxing meal. As they were leaving together, Sarah said, "Any luck apartment hunting?"

"No, nothing yet. If I don't find something quick, I may need to take an offer that a company in Mukilteo gave me. The commute is killing me. That's one of my other conditions—I want to be close to wherever I work. And I'd prefer something close to water. I'm not sure I can explain why—I just like being able to see it."

"Oh, wow, you really thought this out. So, affordable, close to work and water, what else?"

"Well, I'm not settling for, you know, anything less than somewhere I'm proud to say I live. Anyway, thanks for having dinner with me. I really enjoy talking to you. Gotta go jump in my car and get rolling. See you."

Sarah waved good-bye and headed home.

\*\*\*\*\*\*

For the next three weeks, they met each Friday at the Lockspot and had dinner together. Each meal seemed to get a little longer. She learned all about him, including that he was two years older than her and had been in a few short-term relationships that didn't seem to go anywhere. Somewhere in the conversations, Sarah always asked about his apartment search. Each time she did, he added more criteria to his quest.

After what had become their fourth dinner date, it was time to say good night. Standing outside the restaurant, Wade took a step closer to her and said, "I, um—look, I heard some things I didn't mean to a while ago and I know you were in a long relationship and, well, he left and it was hard for you. I just wanted to say, I get it, and I really enjoy your company, but I figure you aren't ready for romance and I'm happy to be a friend."

"What are you saying, Wade?" Sarah asked.

"Well, I can't find an apartment anywhere around here and I think I'm going to take that other job up north. So, well, you have my number, and I was hoping we could still get together now and then and maybe…well, there's no maybe really, I just wanted to let you know."

"When are you leaving?"

Mumbling a bit, he said, "Actually, I gave my two-week notice yesterday."

"Maybe you could give your search a bit more time." Sarah suggested. Thinking fast, she decided to emphasize how challenging his search was. "I mean, you want something you can afford; that's nice looking; near a bus stop; that's preferably a corner unit so the place has a lot of light, not with only eastern exposure because then you wouldn't have the right light; with a high walking score in the area; that's over seven hundred square feet of space, I think you said; with walls painted white; in a quiet building; with a one-year lease and month-to-month after that; and with free rent for the first month. Is that everything?"

Wade thought about it for a moment and said, "Well, I know that's a lot, but yeah, I think that's everything."

Sarah started to say something, but Wade interrupted her. "Actually, there is one more thing. I'd like a view too. Something that would, you know, inspire me."

Rolling her eyes, Sarah said, "Well, good luck in Mukilteo, I guess."

"I'll still be here next Friday," Wade said, a bit sheepishly. "Do you still want to have a bite to eat with me?"

"Sure, of course," she replied, images of their last meal together flying through her head.

\*\*\*\*\*\*

Sarah woke up Saturday morning, inspired by an ambitious plan that seemed to be half dream and half solid idea. She spent the rest of Saturday and Sunday working on it.

Reporting for work in the morning on Monday, she went straight to her post. Today she was filling in at the admissions desk for a half shift before she returned to her usual job in the Collections Department. She worked until her lunch break at twelve thirty. When she was relieved, she headed straight to the accounting office and knocked on Wade's door. He was eating his lunch at his desk, paperwork everywhere.

"Sarah! What are you doing here?"

"Here, take this." She handed him a card with an address on it.

He looked it over and said, "What's this?"

"It's my address. Where I live. I'm making you a dinner tonight. Can you be there at six?"

Wade eyed her for a moment and said, "You think a single guy like me would pass up a home-cooked meal?"

Sarah smiled back and said, "See you at six."

The address was the Seaview Place Apartments, quaint firmly-structured buildings, well-kept and clean, very near the Locks. Wade pushed the entry button for 104, and the door buzzed, allowing him in. He got his bearings and found unit 104 right down the first level hall. Before he could knock on the door, Sarah opened it up and welcomed him in.

"Come on in and take your coat off. Make yourself comfortable. I have a drink poured for you already." Sarah handed him his favorite vodka and water and picked up her glass of wine. "So this is my place. What do you think?"

Trying his best to be diplomatic, he said, "I can tell you decorated it. It looks great."

"Liar," Sarah said, laughing. "I did decorate it, but it's small and just a studio, but it's all I can afford."

"I didn't lie," Wade said. "I may have stretched the normal parameters of truthful discourse just a tiny bit, but I wouldn't call that a lie."

"OK, Pinocchio. The apartment's all right, but I'd love more room. Dinner is still cooking and it needs another thirty minutes, so I want you to follow me." She playfully grabbed the middle of his tie and pulled him along with her.

They left her apartment and went down the hall to the elevators. Rising up four floors, they got out and she led him to apartment 401. Using a key, she opened it up and escorted him in. "Take a look at this!"

Warming to the task, Wade wandered through the two-bedroom, two-bath unit. After looking at it, he said, "This is nice." Then, scratching his head, he asked, "Why are you showing it to me?"

"It just became available, and Joanie, who works in the leasing office, told me right away in case I was interested," Sarah replied, smiling. "She's holding it for me for one more day, so you'd have to move fast. Corner unit looking south and west. Lots of light. Bus stop is like forty feet away. Close to work. Close to Puget Sound. High walk score. Almost a thousand square feet. Nice clean place you'd be proud to live at. They'll do a one-year lease, and the first month would be free for you. What do you think?"

Wade shook his head. "Blue walls," he said, smirking a bit.

"You didn't look in the closet," Sarah answered, pointing to the door.

Wade opened it up and spotted four cans of white paint resting on the floor. Laughing, he said, "Very good. But let's be real. I can never afford this. How much do they want?"

"Twenty-two hundred," Sarah replied.

Wade threw his hands up. "That's a no-go, Sar."

Flashing a secret smile, Sarah said, "I know. So that's why I was thinking I'd take the really nice bedroom with the bath and you could take the smaller one with the bathroom down the hall. Could you afford half of it?"

Eyes wide, Wade stuttered and said, "You want to…to move in with me?"

"No, silly. You'd be moving in with *me*. And I'll pay the first month's rent, so that's how you get your free month."

Wade's eyes continued to grow wider. "Sarah, you hardly know me. We aren't, you know…"

Sarah cut him off. "I know. That's why it will work. You've been nothing but kind and respectful of me. You know I had a tough time lately and you didn't ask anything from me. I know I can trust you. What do you say?"

Rubbing his chin a bit, Wade walked over to the south window. "You're forgetting something. I need a view to inspire me."

She grabbed his arm and pulled him over to the west window. "Take a look."

Straining his eyes, Wade stared and then said, "I'm sorry, I'm not seeing anything."

"Well, you're not looking hard enough. Look right where I'm pointing. Between those two trees. See the blue? That tiny sliver is Puget Sound. Water! That's a view if I ever saw one!"

Wade turned and looked at his friend. "Actually, I'd see *you* every morning, wouldn't I?"

Sarah pouted her lips slightly and said, "Your point?"

Wade locked eyes with her and whispered, "I'm feeling inspired already."

Smiling, Sarah thought to herself, *Maybe Kristen was right. Maybe it is the Luckyspot.*

"C'mon, we can talk about it over dinner." She grabbed his tie and pulled him along again.

# STRIVING FOR PERFECTION

Tyler McKay checked his GPS and realized he was well off the expected path. The phone call he received ten minutes ago distracted him greatly, and he knew now that he had taken a wrong turn. He needed to get back to downtown Seattle, and going west on NW 65th wasn't going to get him there.

He turned left onto 24th and headed south toward the next major arterial. As he did, he picked up his phone and started to dial a long distance number. At 60th, he eased over to the right side of the road and claimed a parking spot. He didn't want to make the same mistake again and miss his turn.

"International Manpower," said the voice on the other end.

"Hi, this is Tyler McKay with Beaker's Cafés calling. Can you put me through to Jared Wayne?"

A moment later, he was connected to Beaker's account exec who handled the higher level position fulfillment.

"Jared, how are you doing?"

"I'm doing. What can I do for you?"

"I just got some bad news. The man you recommended we hire to head up our pastry division just took another job with Simmons Bakeries. Simmons! What happened? Aren't we paying enough?" Tyler nearly yelled into the phone.

Jared's exhale could be easily heard on the line. "Oh, no! I'm sorry, Tyler. I thought he was onboard and ready to go."

"Well, go he did," Tyler said, fuming. "Look, I need you to start searching ASAP. I need someone who has the talent, can teach, is committed to excellence, and has a unique vision that dovetails with Beaker's. And I need him tomorrow!"

"Jeez, Tyler, I'll drop everything and work solely on this, but I'll need more time than one day."

Tyler shook his head as he sat alone in his Lexus. "Damn it, Jared. We've scheduled a press conference for tomorrow and planned to unveil the new concepts in pastries that we have and introduce our new guy. Now I'm going to have to punt unless you come up with someone. Someone with a vision and the ability to express it, OK?"

Jared promised again to work full boar on it, but Tyler didn't feel confident. He rang off and sat still in the driver's seat for thirty seconds, thinking. When no answers came to him, he realized he was hungry and looked around him. There, not forty feet from where he was parked, stood a French eatery called the Café Besalu. He walked in and looked around.

Immediately a young woman smiled and said, "Welcome! What can I get for you?"

Liking the vibe already, he took a closer look at the items offered at the counter and said, "I think I'd like to try a Loraine quiche, and let me have one of those cardamom twists too."

"Coffee?" the young woman asked. "We have multiple new blends."

"Yes," Tyler said, "of course. Pick out a blend for me that goes with what I ordered."

The young lady's eyes lit up, and she said, "Glad to. You'll like it."

Tyler paid and grabbed the last table available in the room. People kept filing in as he waited.

Nine minutes later, the young woman brought Tyler's order over to his table. "Anything else I can get you?"

"No, this looks really good. What's your name?"

"I'm Beth, Beth Harding." She extended her hand along with her ever-present smile.

"Tyler McKay, with Beaker's Cafés. I just stumbled on your place and—" He took a bite of the quiche and stopped talking. "Oh! Oh, this is very good. Excellent. What's your role here?"

Beth rolled her eyes. "What isn't it? Manager, cook, accountant, chief bottle-washer, and janitor," she said, laughing. "It's OK. I love it."

Still eating, Tyler egged her on between mouthfuls. "What do you like about it?"

"My boss gave me the freedom to experiment a bit and try to make the pastries and menu items tastier and more attractive. I love doing that. I combine unique foods together and try new cooking methods and, you know, strive for perfection."

Tyler's curiosity was growing. "Do you have a degree? Are you a chef?"

"I graduated from the UW Business Admin school eight years ago, but went—oh, excuse me, customers come before chit-chat, sorry." She hurried back behind the counter to assist a young male employee who was looking overwhelmed. A few minutes later, she returned to Tyler's table.

"I see that quiche is gone," she noted.

"It was the best I've ever had," Tyler said, with a surprising sincerity. He rarely gave strong compliments, but this one simply slipped out. He picked up the twist and took a bite of that as well. He paused as he enjoyed the pastry's utter perfection.

Looking back at Beth, he asked, "What did you say before? You strive for, um, excellence?"

Beth shook her head. "No. I strive for perfection."

Tyler gave her a slight grin. "Perfection, huh? That's a tall order. Sometimes in business you have to settle for less and try again another day."

"I know, but I don't think it's right to have any other goal. I want my croissants, my pretzels, quiches, cinnamon rolls, and everything else I make to be so tasty, so delicious that even the busiest person in the world takes the first bite and closes their eyes and thinks of nothing else. I want my creations to be so good that it helps our customers to escape from their daily troubles, if only for a few moments, and lets them luxuriate in culinary bliss. If I make something and I don't see a hint of that special moment on their face, then I failed. And I hate failing, so I keep working on it."

Tyler stared at her, the awe in his eyes far too evident.

Blushing a bit, Beth laughed and said, "Oh, my. I got carried away there. Sorry." She gave a friendly wave and returned to the counter to check on her protégé. He whispered something to her about his job and laughed. She laughed with him, displaying a genuine touch for communicating with her employees.

Thinking fast, Tyler finished his twist and his coffee and waited until she was manning the counter by herself. He rose, walked over, and said, "I've got kind of a sweet tooth. Got anything you'd recommend for dessert—something I can take out? And another coffee as well."

Beth's eyes twinkled, and she said, "I know just the thing. It's something we call an Aprichoc croissant. A little fruit and a little chocolate together. You want the same blend of coffee?"

"No, please choose the coffee again for me again. Something to go with the dessert," Tyler said.

"OK, but don't drive and eat at the same time. You'll close your eyes to reach the peak of nirvana with this combination," Beth said, only half teasing. "You might have an accident. Wouldn't want that."

Tyler laughed and nodded. "I'll be careful. You never told me, Beth. Did you study to become a chef?"

"I grew up working under a slew of Ballard's finest while I put myself through school. I guess some folks would call me a chef. I prefer experimenter-in-chief."

"And this is where you choose to work? This is a fine place, but I think you could do better. I have a job I'd like to interview you for, and it would give you far more responsibility, far more money, and the opportunity to impact millions instead of hundreds. Would you like to learn more?"

A man and his wife walked in the front door and made eye contact with Beth. She lit up and said, "Don! Barbara! Good to see you. The usual?"

"You betcha," they said in tandem as they seated themselves at Tyler's old table.

"I love Ballard, Mr. McKay," Beth answered. "And I'm happy here. Can you promise me all those things you mentioned and guarantee me I'll be happy too?"

"I, well, I can say this," Tyler began. "You'd be happy with the challenges and the opportunity. I mean, really, who can promise happiness?"

Beth winked at him. "At least you're truthful. Being happy is more important to me right now, and I am deliriously happy right here in Ballard. Check back with me in a year or two, if you like. Maybe I'll have reached perfection here and be ready for something else."

Recognizing defeat when it slapped him in the face, Tyler smiled and said, "I'll be back. I think you would be exactly what we need to spread some culinary bliss around the whole world."

He nodded his good-bye to her and returned to his car. Seated there, the CEO and chairman of the board of Beaker's Worldwide Coffee Services took a taste of the Aprichoc croissant and pressed his eyes closed as he forgot about everything else.

# THE RETURN

Lori Westfall couldn't help but smile as she gazed from the bus window at her beloved Ballard. She couldn't remember how long it had been since she last returned to the community. She'd grown up here and her memory was foggy, but she knew it had been quite a long time.

The views were definitely different. She knew that Ballard had changed greatly during her absence, but she still marveled over all the new buildings and how busy and bustling the area was now.

The bus came to the intersection of Market and 15th, and she looked all around but couldn't see the old Denny's. *Wasn't it on the corner? I remember Dad taking me there, and we'd sit at the counter and each have a dish full of Jell-O cubes. My favorite was red. Dad would always have green. Jeez, I remember that like it was yesterday. Now I can't even find the Denny's.*

The bus pulled to the curb on Market just past Bartell's, and she exited along with many other people. She was amazed at how easy it was to get on and off the bus.

She took her time, strolling west on Market. She passed a 7-Eleven that she vaguely remembered. *Was it here when we lived here? I can't remember now.*

Across the street was a donut shop called the Mighty O. She smiled to herself and was tempted to cross the street and sample her favorite, a big bear claw, but she decided she would wait until later.

So busy looking around, she almost bumped into a woman pushing a carriage. Lori stepped to the side at the last minute and said, "Sorry, didn't see you."

She continued down Market toward 20th Avenue. She passed several businesses she didn't remember, but then, laughing, she gave herself a free pass. *Lori, you were only eight years old when you lived here. Of course you didn't take notice of businesses—unless they were selling candy or ice cream.*

At 20th, she turned right, and she realized she had done that many times when she was young. She passed Golden City, a Chinese restaurant she felt she might remember, and suddenly she was sure that her parents' home had been very near. As she arrived at NW 56th, she felt a familiar excitement.

"That building, on the north side of the street, is new," she said to herself. "The Vik—whatever that is. Apartments or something. But up ahead, on the left, that's where our house is. I'm pretty sure." Lori walked farther and saw a few small buildings but nothing that resembled her memory of their house. The second half of the street was taken up by huge buildings on both sides.

"Maybe I was wrong. I don't see our house here. Maybe it's on the next street." She turned around and walked back to 20th. Heading north, she turned on 57th and found many more houses there, but none were the one she lived in. Convinced she got her street address confused, she decided to just explore and see what else she could find.

She walked past the Common's Park and spotted a young man standing in the middle of the park, looking around this way and that. He made eye contact with her and waved.

*OK, I don't know this guy, but he sort of looks familiar, and this is Ballard. It's friendly, right?* She gave him a slight wave back, and he instantly reacted with a smile. She kept on walking.

At 24th, she turned left and walked back to 56th. Still convinced that their home was on that street, she headed east on it and looked for her house. She recognized nothing. All the buildings seemed so new. She crossed 22nd and saw the library. She had gone to the library before with her mother, but she didn't remember it looking like this one.

Continuing up 56th, she noticed a large, modern police car parked in the lot. Looking harder, it appeared that two officers were inside. Smiling, she walked to the driver's side where the window was already down and said, "Hi, I was wondered if you could give me some directions? I was looking—"

Before she could finish, a crackle erupted from the police radio. A woman talking in police codes, seemingly with a sense of urgency, called out, and suddenly both officers started moving. The driver hit a switch and the emergency roof lights came on, and without so much as a word, the car sped off, turning west on 56th and flying through the 22nd Avenue intersection.

Lori just stood there. "Yow! Excuse us, miss, we have to go!" she said to herself, pretending the officers had the manners to address her before they sped off. *This isn't like the Ballard I remember. We loved living here, but everyone seems so busy now. I'm not sure I like it. I'm just going to find our old home and go. Maybe if I—*

She stopped her thought midsentence. There was the man from the park again, standing across the street, staring intently at her. He waved again.

Not sure what to do, she tried to ignore him. Leaving the library parking lot, Lori headed east again in search of her home. The man crossed to her side of the street and walked rapidly behind her, trying to catch up.

Having had enough of this, Lori spun around and confronted him. "What's your problem? I don't know you. What do you want?"

The man froze in his tracks. A car drove by slowly, and for just a moment, Lori thought about flagging him down. A second's hesitation cost her the opportunity, as the driver passed by without giving her as much as a glance.

"I'm sorry. I was looking for someone," the man said.

"Well, quit following me. It's, um, bad manners," Lori said.

The man started to turn away, but then turned back to her and said, "Look, I'm kind of in new territory here too. All I know is I think, well, I mean I—"

"Spit it out!" she yelled, fearful of what he might say or do.

"OK, sorry. Are you…are you Lori?"

It was Lori's turn to freeze. *How could he know my name? Nobody knows me here.* She didn't answer him. Instead she asked, "Who are you?"

The man gulped and said, "You don't recognize me, do you? I mean, I can't blame you. Look at me. I'm so young."

"What are you talking about?" Lori said, exasperated.

"Lori, it's Dad. I don't know how I got here, but I'm here to take you, you know, home."

"I can't find my home," Lori blurted out, eyes filling with tears. "Who? You're not—"

"Honey, we aren't part of this world anymore. They can't even see us. Nothing is the same. We've both passed."

"You mean…? Oh! Oh, my! The accident. I remember the brakes didn't—"

"Don't worry about that now. I'm supposed to guide you up."

"Up?"

The man smiled and suddenly she could see her father's younger self, his eyes twinkling the same way they did as they sat at the counter and ate their Jell-O. "Daddy!" she cried. She melted into his arms, and they were gone.

# JASON'S TREASURE

A stack of bills rested on Jason Lindberg's desk. He stared at it, then shifted his gaze to the stack of checks that were supposed to come in today, but didn't. Jason was thirty-eight and owned his own business—a kitchen and catering service in a building just off of Leary Way. He had quit his full-time job eighteen months ago and used his life savings to buy the business. It was doing well for the previous owner, but after Jason took over things got steadily worse. Sales slacked off, turnover increased, his sales rep quit, and the new rental agreement he had to sign didn't go in his favor. On top of that, Nona, his chef and kitchen manager, gave him her one-month notice, saying she just didn't like the work anymore. Finding another chef as good as Nona would be exceedingly difficult.

Now, as a first-time business owner, he was losing money each month. He paid himself the same as the previous owner during the first year, but now hadn't paid himself for the last five months. If it weren't for the love of his life, Emily, making good money along with great benefits as a paralegal, they would be in dire straits.

Jason contemplated the situation and knew he was going to have to take drastic action rapidly. He'd already laid off four people in his crew of twenty and nearly half of those remaining were brand new. Staring again at the stack of bills, he thought, *If I don't come up with a plan quickly, we're screwed. I know buying lotto tickets isn't really a plan, so I've got to come up with something else.*

Two weeks later, with sales dipping further, he went into a tirade in the office and fired three more workers who were making rookie mistakes and teeing off some large customers. Jason dismissed them and stormed out of the building. He went to Mike's Chili Parlor on Ballard Way, near 15th Northwest, and ordered a bourbon neat with a beer chaser.

He sat on a stool at the bar for nearly an hour, nursing both drinks, racking his brain, trying to come up with an idea for how to turn the business around. Nothing was coming to him.

As he was about to leave, an older gentleman sat down next to him and glanced at Jason's drinks. He ordered the same from the bartender.

Jason looked at the silver-haired man and asked, "You looking for some answers too?"

"Won't find any answers here, son. And never in the bottom of a cup."

Pondering that, Jason replied, "I can't find them anywhere else either. My business is falling apart and I don't know what to do."

The man offered his hand. "I'm Thomas. I'm retired now, but I've owned a few businesses in my time and I know how hard it can be. Tell me your name."

Rapidly Jason thrust his hand forward, saying, "I'm Jason, Jason Lindberg, and I own Lindberg Catering."

"Can't say I've heard of it," Thomas said.

"Used to be called Mortenson Deluxe Catering, and it was very successful," Jason replied.

"That was your first mistake. Changing the name," Thomas said.

"Well, it's *my* business. I should have *my* name on it," Jason protested.

"Yup, you should. Eventually. But I remember that Mortenson name, so when you changed it, you lost all the goodwill they had built up. And you broadcasted to everyone that a new sheriff was in town, and they loved the old one. The time to change the name is after you've built up more clients and everyone knows you."

"I didn't think of that," Jason said, his head hanging a bit lower.

"Common mistake. You can overcome that. Tell me more about your problem."

Moving to a table, Jason and Thomas ordered some chili and fries and talked deep into the night. Jason told him what he had done to try to turn things around. When he was done, Thomas mulled it over for a few minutes.

Turning to his dinner partner, Thomas said, "So let me summarize. You started running into cash flow problems within eight months, but you kept paying yourself first and everything else second. You went back to your vendors and tried to cut better deals. When you couldn't, you went out and signed new contracts with vendors who sold you lower quality food at lower costs. You froze pay levels on everybody and threatened them with layoffs if they didn't work harder. You didn't—"

"When you put it that way, it sounds terrible. I had to do something," Jason interrupted.

Thomas looked at him closely with steely gray eyes. "I'm not done yet; let me finish."

Jason realized he was being defensive.

Thomas continued, "You didn't hire a new sales rep, and now your head chef has given her notice. Now the bank wants its loan paid back, and you don't have the money. Does that about sum it up?"

Jason simply nodded. There wasn't much fight left in him.

"How much do you need to take care of the bank?"

"Twenty-five thousand."

"And how much do you need to catch all your bills up and get current?" Thomas asked.

Jason thought for a moment and caught himself just before he started to count the thousands on his fingers. "Probably another twenty."

"Young man, you'll need working capital, too. Probably another twenty. So here's what I'll do. I'll loan you sixty-five thousand dollars so you can keep operating on the condition that you bring back your chef by offering her a raise and autonomy in picking vendors and new hires. Will you do that?"

Jason shook his head. "It's *my* company. I get to hire people. And she won't come back. She doesn't like the work anymore."

Thomas nodded and said, "Jason, you're getting your ego all mixed up in this. I can't help you, then." He started to get up from the table.

"Wait! I'll try to do what you say. I need the loan."

"Wrong answer, son."

"Well, what do you want from me?"

"Jason," Thomas said, sounding more like a father than a business partner. "You have to bring your game up a bit. I know this is your first business to run, but you have to recognize what's important. You're sitting on a treasure and you're not protecting it. And when I offered you the money, you never asked what it would cost you."

"Oh, gawd! I'm terrible at this. There's so much I don't know. OK, what will it cost me?"

"I'll charge you eleven percent interest because you have no collateral, and that is a steal in itself. But after you pay it off, I want you to sell me ten percent of the company for a dollar."

"Deal!" Jason said, far too eagerly.

"OK, not so fast," Thomas chided. "First of all, I'm going to have to teach you a bit about negotiating. You should have countered, say, nine percent interest and five percent of the business. You have to show a financier that you believe in yourself and that you think your company is worth more than that."

Jason buried his head in his hands. He stifled a sob and said, "I have no clue what I'm doing, do I?"

Thomas chuckled. "That's OK, this is the way most entrepreneurs learn. I'm going to order one more drink for both of us, then I'm going to ask you a question. You get one chance at answering correctly, and if you don't, well, I wish you good luck."

Jason finished his fries and said, "Sounds like I'm up against it."

"Son, you were up against it from day one," Thomas said. "But you have two things going for you. You had the nerve to quit a good job and go out on your own. You were brave enough to do that. I admire that in any man or woman."

"What's the other thing?" Jason asked.

"That's what you have to figure out. That's your one question. You think on that while I go order us one more drink."

As Thomas started to get up, Mike, the owner, came by and asked, "Can I get you two something else?"

Thomas nodded and said, "A couple of Cokes, please. We're wrapping it up here."

Moments later, Mike returned with two Cokes. "These are on me, gents. Looks like you're making some progress here."

"Thanks, Mike. I think we are," Thomas said.

Jason accepted his Coke and stared back at Thomas. "Thank you, sir. I appreciate all you've done."

That said, Jason disappeared back into himself, trying to figure out the one other thing he had going for him.

They both sipped their drinks slowly in silence.

Jason looked up at him and asked, "Could you repeat the question again?"

"Besides your own nerve to buy the business and start to build your own life, tell me what you think is the thing of greatest value in your business. Think about it, Jason. The answer to this question, in my mind and in my experience, is true for virtually any business. It's where the treasure of your business lies. What is your treasure, Jason?"

Jason took a deep breath and said, "OK, I'm not answering yet. I just have to talk this out loud, like I would with my wife."

"Very good idea. Go ahead. Do a little inventory of all you have. I have a good poker face, so if you say the right thing, you'll get no reaction from me. Just think it out."

"OK, OK," he started nervously. "I've got a good customer list. Still some regular customers that keep ordering. That's pretty valuable. And I've got Nona, if I can bring her back, and there are a few others that try hard. I've got a lot of used equipment that is valuable and…and hell, who am I kidding? Reselling that would be hard, and I need it, so I'd only sell it if I closed down."

Jason paused for a moment. He wiped the sweat off his brow as he realized his answer would doom him or save him.

"I don't have a good sales guy anymore. I don't have much cash in the bank. I have my wife who is a super help when it comes to thinking things out, and she has some great ideas about marketing, but they all take money. I have a new lease, but I know that isn't it. One thing, you say, right? One thing that most businesses have that is a treasure?"

Patiently, Thomas nodded. He took another sip of his drink.

Jason noticed that it was half empty—or half full. *Depends on your point of view,* he thought. The irony of the situation wasn't lost on him

"OK, I think I know. Now that I think about it, there is one thing that is more important than all the others," Jason said, then downed another gulp of his drink.

123

Swallowing hard, he looked Thomas in the eyes and said, "It's my employees, isn't it?"

Thomas let his poker face stay in place, milking the moment. He slowly took another sip of his drink, then said, "See, you do have what it takes to win."

Jason nearly collapsed on the table. Smiling broadly, chuckling a bit, he said, "I don't know why I didn't see it before. They were used to working for Mr. Mortenson. They didn't like me because I kept trying to save money by cutting their pay and getting rid of the best people, to cut costs faster."

Thomas nodded. "Correct. And Nona isn't tired of the work. She's probably just tired of you. I bet she likes being a chef. And I bet she liked the autonomy that the previous owner gave her. She's proven herself. Give her some control over her people and get out of her way. Offer her the same pay as before, but set some goals for her and pay her a bonus every month. Let her bring her own people in and give them bonuses too. While she's running the kitchen, you can go out and sell to old customers and new ones. Admit that you made some mistakes and you're going back to doing the same things the Mortensons did. I bet you'll win those customers back. Later we can show better numbers to the bank and get your loan extended to ease cash flow. But, first and foremost, you take good care of your treasure—every employee you've got. In return, they'll take care of the business."

Jason shook as he tried to hold his laughter inside, the relief pouring over him like a waterfall.

Finally he said, "Oh, man. I am one lucky dude. I was ready to give up, and by pure chance, you sat right beside me and turned out to be the one I needed."

"Actually," Thomas said, "not quite so pure."

Jason's eyes widened. "What do you mean?"

"I mean I wasn't just passing by," Thomas said, smiling.

"How…what?" Jason started stuttering.

"Your wife called for you at the office, and Nona told her that you stormed out. She guessed you were going to a bar. Your wife is one smart cookie. She knew you'd be here. See, Emily used to work with me at the law firm. I was a managing partner. She called and asked me to come down and give you some business advice."

"You gave me more than that," Jason said.

"Yeah," Thomas said, staring off in the distance. "I wonder...I wonder if that was her plan all along."

"Emily's pretty smart," Jason said, still smiling.

"All the better for us," Thomas said. "I think the three of us will make a great partnership."

As they left the bar, Jason said, "Is it too late to change my answer? Maybe Emily is really my greatest treasure."

Thomas laughed. "I think you're on to something there."

# 22nd AND MARKET

Kay Reynolds stood at the bus stop on 24th chatting with Carl and Sandy. They had caught the 40 going downtown at the same time for more than five years. Today was a cold Monday in October, and they chose to stand and move a bit to keep themselves warm. Ben, Ray, and Maggie were seated on the bench, hunkering down in their warm coats.

Kay knew just about everybody who rode the 40. She had been boarding it for seven years, heading for her job working for the city in the Street Use Department. She was twenty-eight, five-foot-seven, bright green eyes that were the highlight of her face, and auburn hair that fell to her shoulders. She was single and growing tired of it. There had been no new and interesting faces joining the department lately, and she yearned to meet someone who could win her heart. Long ago she'd decided that man would have to be educated, ambitious, travel-minded, kind, and, more than anything else, a fun person to be around. Those were her objectives, and she figured if she could stay young and eligible for another hundred and fifty years, she just might meet him.

The 40 arrived on time as usual, and the driver watched as nearly everyone flashed their card and boarded. Kay always took one of the sideways seats, always in the middle, so she would have a friend sitting on each side. Knowing nearly everyone's first name made it a friendly, almost intimate ride with different people every day.

The 40 turned left onto Market and rolled on up to 22nd, where a swarm of people boarded. Kay knew them too. Rarely did anyone board that Kay had not seen before. Most nodded to her and others as they passed. Sometimes someone from 22nd would sit down in an open spot next to her and chat on the way into the city.

Today was different though. After nearly everyone from 22nd had boarded, a tall man she had never seen before boarded the bus and, for a millisecond, made eye contact with her before he passed by looking for an open seat. He found one way in the back of the bus and grabbed it while he could.

"There's a new one," Edna whispered, leaning over toward Kay's ear.

"Probably a onesy," Kay said, using the word they coined for riders who never showed up again. Smiling to herself, she thought, *It's always good to see someone new. I'm for anything that breaks the drudging monotony of the same ole, same ole.*

Over the next few days, the tall man continued to board at 22nd. He always wore a suit and tie, his shoes were polished, and his short hair was perfectly in place. And he always made eye contact with Kay. On Thursday that week, he glanced at her as he passed and gave her a brief nod. On Friday, she got both a nod and a small smile.

Patsy sat on Kay's left, and after he passed, she said, "Hmm, I don't see any wedding ring on that one. I think he likes you."

Kay chuckled. "Maybe he likes you, Patsy."

"Nice try. I could be his grandma. No, he's looking at you. I'm sure."

Ron, an accountant who was nearing retirement, sat on Kay's other side. "One way to find out. If he's on again next week, I'll sit near him and get some intel for you."

"You don't have to do that, Ron," Kay replied.

"Why not? It'll be fun. I always wanted to be a secret agent. You know, gathering prized bits of information as a spy behind enemy lines."

Kay rolled her eyes. "I don't think it will end well for you. Most spies meet an untimely demise."

Ron laughed. "I'll try not to get shot."

Monday arrived and Kay found herself strangely excited to see if the stranger would board the bus again. He did. Ron was already in the back of the bus, standing, waiting for his chance. The man took the only window seat remaining and Ron slid in next to him.

On Tuesday, Ron boarded at 22nd and sat beside Kay in the front sideways seat. Again the man boarded, nearly arriving too late to catch the bus. Hurriedly, he glanced at Kay and, making no nod or smile, passed by, sitting four rows past her on the same side.

Ron leaned over and whispered to her, "His name is Wally. He's a detective with the Seattle police. Not married. Just moved to Seattle from Denver. Seems like a nice fella."

"Wally?" Kay asked, her face a bit askew.

"Well, I'm sure it's Walter, but he's probably a casual kind of guy," Ron offered.

Jeanine, a thirtysomething concierge at a classy hotel downtown, sat opposite Kay on the other side of the bus. She leaned over and said, "I know what's going on. I'll get some more info tomorrow. I know lots of tricks for getting men to talk."

Kay started to protest, but her seatmates stifled her and gave a subtle thumbs up to Jeanine.

On Thursday, Jeanine sat next to Kay and immediately leaned over and said, "You're not going to believe what I found out."

Kay's eyes widened as she whispered back, "Maybe I shouldn't know. I don't think we should really be—"

"Shush!" Jeanine said, cutting her off. "Here he comes."

Wally made solid eye contact this time with Kay, nodded distinctively, and smiled. He sat three rows back of her by the window.

Glancing his way, Kay spotted her friend Maggie sliding into the open seat next to him, trying hard to hide an excited smile. *This is getting out of control,* Kay thought.

Jeanine was nearly foaming at the mouth to tell her what she found out. "So listen to this," she began. "I introduced myself and he did too. He said his name is Andrew. Not Walter or whatever Ron heard. He says he's a tax attorney for a new firm in Seattle. He's married and has four kids. Four!"

"What? But Ron said—"

"I think he's lying. Look at the way he dresses. I think he really *is* a detective," Jeanine said, cutting Kay off again. "Maybe he's under cover. This could be really exciting." For the rest of the ride into town, Jeanine talked nonstop about all the possibilities. Kay pressed her eyes closed and fervently wished to be somewhere else.

The next day, Maggie sat next to Kay and told her what she had learned. "His name is Ricardo. He's from Brazil, he's American, and he's a coffee salesman up here meeting with Starbucks. He's thirty-two and gay. He loves horror films and says his favorite food is cotton candy. Can you believe it?"

"Which part?" Kay deadpanned.

"Cotton candy!" Maggie exclaimed. "Who lists that as their favorite food?"

Kay stared at the roof of the bus. She knew he was sitting just two rows away on the opposite side, and she had a feeling he was watching her.

The following week was filled with one person after another sitting next to her, filling her in on all they found out about him. His name was Troy, Benjamin, Marvin. He was single, gay, married with kids, married with three wives in Algeria, a celibate monk. He was unemployed; he was a mattress salesman, a diamond merchant. His hobby was coin collecting, making homemade beer, studying abstract painting. By Friday of that week, he was seated only one row behind her on the opposite side. He would smile, amused by Kay's attempt to not listen to the myriad of stories coming at her.

On the following Monday, she waited at the stop on 24th with all her friends. Addressing everyone, she said, "Look, this needs to stop. I don't want anyone else bothering Wally or whatever his name is. Please, no more. This is embarrassing. I'm going to put a stop to it today. Carl, I want you on my right, and Sandy, you're on my left. When he boards the bus, I want both of you to get up and move to another seat somewhere else. I'm going to point to him and make sure he sits down next to me. Then I'm going to clear this silliness all up. Probably make a damn fool of myself in the process, but I'm not doing this anymore, OK? Got it?"

Stunned by demure Kay's outburst, they all nodded.

The 40 came by, picking them all up. Kay sat on the sideways seat flanked by Carl and Sandy as instructed. The bus arrived at the 22nd stop. Everyone boarded. The mystery man, as everyone had started to call him, never got on board. He was a no show on Tuesday as well. He was nowhere to be found for the rest of the week.

Perplexed and somewhat disappointed, Kay joined her friends at the stop on the last Monday in October. They all had their umbrellas out as dark clouds emptied their liquid treasure all morning long.

Idling next to Kay, Sandy spoke from under her umbrella. "You look down."

Kay lifted her umbrella's angle up a bit to meet Sandy's eyes. "I guess I was, I don't know, sort of looking forward to seeing him again. You know, just to clear the air and find out what his real story is."

Sandy smiled. "It *was* kind of exciting, wasn't it?"

"Well, I guess so," Kay agreed. "I mean, we do the same thing every day and a little break in the monotony can be fun. Well, fun until it became embarrassing, that is."

"He probably bought a car, or switched to Uber or something. He never looked like a bus person to me. Too well dressed," Sandy suggested.

Kay just nodded.

The 40 pulled up and Sandy got on first, followed by Kay. She paid with her card and looked up to see her usual sideways seat taken already by a man holding a newspaper in front of his face. He lowered and folded it in his lap.

Kay stopped short, and the woman behind her bumped in to her. The mystery man pointed to the seat beside himself and said, "Care to join me?"

Cautiously, Kay sat down. The man moved over a few inches so that it became unlikely that a third rider would try to squeeze in.

Smiling disarmingly, the man said, "I thought we should talk. I have an apology to make."

"You do?" Kay asked.

"Yeah, I'm not very nice sometimes. I played a rotten trick on you. I mean, I usually fib a bit when it's not important, just to have some fun. Then I saw that whatever I told that fellow, Ron, he was telling you. After that, well, it was almost too easy to get some laughs."

"Wait a minute," Kay said, holding her hand up like a stop sign. "First of all, what the heck is your name? Your real name."

Chuckling a bit, he said, "Good place to start. My name is Holden. Holden Russell. And, yeah, before you ask, yes, my parents named me Holden because they both liked that tragic hero of *Catcher in the Rye*, Holden Caulfield."

Kay looked at him closely. He was a calm person, still dressed well, with an average face and build. Not a movie star, but not hard to look at either. "Are you tragic?"

"Nope. Not a hero either. You're Kay, right?"

A bit discomfited, realizing that she hadn't reciprocated with her own introduction, Kay quickly said, "Yes, I'm sorry. I'm Kay. Kay Reynolds. So you thought all this was funny, huh?"

"Well, breaks the monotony anyway," Holden said, as Kay eyed him.

"So where were you last week?" Kay asked.

"Took a quick trip to Tokyo. I work as a public defender, and I had a week of vacation time coming and I've never been to Japan, so I went to check it out."

"Just like that? What about the wife and kids?"

"I kinda made that up," Holden admitted.

Kay mulled that over and followed up. "So you're single? And you just up and went to Japan?"

Holden chuckled. "Single as can be. Saw some sights, had some laughs, drank some sake, got lost more than once. I like doing that kind of thing."

Every eye on the bus was straining to see what was happening on the sideways seats on the driver's side. Every ear was cocked in their direction, hoping to steal a snippet of their conversation. The whole bus was eerily silent.

Holden looked around just as Kay did, certain that the two of them had nary an ounce of privacy in this conversation.

Holden started to say something when suddenly Kay slapped her forehead and said, "Wait just a minute here. Am I supposed to fall for this again? How do I know you're really Holden or whatever you said?"

Nodding his agreement, Holden replied, "A very understandable and prudent question. I can show you my driver's license. Would that work?"

Kay agreed, "Yeah, And I'd like to see a business card too."

Reaching for his back pocket and suddenly appearing concerned, Holden said, "Oh, wow, bad timing. It appears I've left my wallet at home."

Kay threw her arms up in the air and said, "You are just full of—"

She stopped when Holden removed his wallet from his suit coat pocket and started laughing. "Got ya!" Then he looked at the rest of the busload of people and pointed to all of them. "Got you, too!"

Everyone laughed.

Holden leaned over and whispered into Kay's ear, "Clearly this is kind of a tough place for us to talk. I do have an apology for you, but you'll have to let me buy you dinner tonight to hear it. Say seven o'clock at the Stoneburner?"

Kay smiled and turned to look into his eyes. Quietly, she answered, "Not on your life. Not until I see some ID."

Holden pulled a business card out of his wallet and passed it to her. It identified him as Holden Russell, Public Defender.

Kay thought about how easy it would be to make up a phony business card. "How about that driver's license?"

Holden flipped his wallet open to display his driver's license. It listed him as Holden N. Russell.

"What's the *n* for?" she asked.

"Never a dull moment."

The 40 was downtown already in what seemed like record time. Kay rose from her seat to get off at her stop. Smiling back at Holden, she said, "See you at seven."

# SHILSHOLE SUNSETS

Amanda carefully dipped her brush into the orange paint bottle and lightly smeared it with a touch of pink from her palette. Satisfied that it was as close as she was going to get to tonight's color, she applied it in fine smooth strokes to the area slightly above the Olympic Mountains. The statue of Leif Erickson stood in the foreground, reflecting the light from behind. And she loved the way the Two Brothers stood so firmly and proudly above the rest of the mountains, as if they alone could reach up and touch the colorful tapestry of art that was tonight's sunset.

Admiring her creation, knowing it may be the last one, she dawdled for a few extra moments, examining her work and then the sunset, which was already changing hue as the sun came closer to hiding once again behind the mountains.

*Can't hide from me*, Amanda thought. *Too late. I captured you already for all time right here on my canvas.*

She smiled to herself and turned her head as much as she could to the left, raised her left arm in a half-wave, and signaled her parents sitting in the car twenty feet from her.

Ellen got out first and beamed at her daughter from twenty feet away, genuinely excited to see the final masterpiece of the month. Every night in this month of September, her parents had driven Amanda out to Shilshole to witness and paint the sunset. Some nights had been nothing but clouds and darkness, yet her talented daughter somehow captured the magic of those evenings as well as she did tonight's brilliant sunset.

"I can't wait to see this one," she mumbled to herself as she hurried closer.

Even Amanda, ever the most hardened critic of her own work, couldn't contain herself. She beamed her crooked smile back at her mother and replied, "Anyone could've done this one tonight. It almost painted itself."

Her mother stood behind her and looked over the artwork. Quietly, almost in a whisper, she said, "I see a lot of love in this one."

Amanda's father, Ed, arrived and leaned over, kissing the top of his daughter's head. "You nailed it, Mandy. It's the best one yet."

Amanda laughed. "You say that every time, Dad."

"And I mean it every time too," he countered.

Carefully removing the canvas from the easel, her father carried it back to the van and secured it safely, as he had with the other twenty-nine. Her mother carried the remaining equipment back and loaded it into the vehicle beside the painting.

"I'm glad this is done," Ellen said. "It took a lot out of her. Her whole left arm is shaking now. She needs to rest."

Ed nodded, saying nothing.

They both returned to their daughter, and Ellen asked, "Ready to go?"

"I'm so glad I got a good one for the last one," Amanda said, trying but failing to turn far enough to the right to see her mother.

"Let's get you home," Ellen said.

Her father turned her wheelchair around and pushed it carefully into the parking lot. They moved to the van and activated the side lift so they could move her and the chair into the vehicle. Once she was secure, he smoothly eased out of the lot and headed to their home on NW 57th.

Over the last two months, Ellen and Ed had met together with multiple venues in Ballard, trying to find the best site for the event that Amanda's passion drove her toward. With fiery determination in what was left of her damaged and crippled body, Amanda had pushed them to help her find a way to contribute to the spinal injury cause. Ellen and Ed kept searching for the right venue, hoping to find a way to stay within their own meager budget.

Today they had a meeting at the Nordic Museum. With multiple different-sized meeting rooms available, they sat down with Bridget, the event coordinator, and explained their plan.

"You see, our daughter was always a talented painter," Ellen said, "but she was also a star athlete at Ballard High, and she spread her many talents far too thin. Three years ago, she was in a horrific car accident that severed her spine and paralyzed her on her right side. Unable to walk or even move normally, she returned to painting, albeit left-handed painting. Over time, she became quite efficient at it. She paints quite well, but, frankly, well…"

Ellen went quiet as she tried to recompose herself. She glanced at her husband as if to say, "You take it from here. I can't do it."

Ed picked up where his wife left off. "Frankly, we are poor judges of real artistic talent. I can barely draw a recognizable stick person, so I know she didn't inherit her skills from me. Painting with her left hand hinders her as well, and truth is, we have doubts that any of these paintings could fetch any serious sums from buyers. But our daughter is no quitter. She has fight in her. When she was on the Ballard girls basketball team, she brought her team from far behind more than once and—"

Now it was Ed's turn to struggle with emotions.

Ellen shook her head. Trying to lighten the mood in the room, she said, "You and your sports. Nothing makes a grown man cry more than a silly ball game. He still cries every time he talks about Edgar Martinez ripping that double into the left field corner against the Yankees."

"I was there. You would've cried too if you'd been there," Ed answered as he dabbed his eyes.

"What my dear husband was trying to say is that she's a fighter and she won't let go of this idea. She wants to raise tens of thousands of dollars to donate to a spinal injury research foundation. We don't know how to say no, so we're looking for a venue that would have some traffic of its own and would be a place we could afford and host an event and hopefully sell some of the paintings."

"How many does she have to display?" Bridget asked.

Ellen swallowed hard and continued, "Thirty. Amanda's idea was to theme the event. Last month, we drove her out to Shilshole and she painted thirty consecutive days of Ballard sunsets. Rain or shine, she was there. Ed built a little tent for her on the windy or rainy days. There were some great ones and some that were so dark we could hardly see. Somehow, she made them all seem special. Well, at least to us they seem that way. Honestly, we're fearful that no one will buy anything and more fearful about what that will do to her."

Bridget broke eye contact with Ellen, and there was a thick silence in the room. She pushed the rate schedule toward Ellen and said, "I understand. These are our normal rates for the various sized rooms, but as a charity event, I can see about getting a better deal for you. Do you happen to have any pictures of what she intends to display?"

Ed reached into a bag that stood beside his chair and pulled out an album. He passed it over to Bridget and said, "She calls it, logically enough, September Sunsets, and she named each one and etched the date on the bottom of the painting. Kind of hard to see in the picture, but the paintings' titles are at the top of the page."

Bridget paged through the book, stopping occasionally on certain pictures. "Your daughter is a very talented young lady. Let me see what I can do. I have your number. I'll call you tomorrow."

The event came together quickly after that. The museum suggested the event be held in their largest meeting room. An anonymous company stepped forward to host the event on Saturday, the third of November, making it part of the celebration on the 130th anniversary of the day Ballard was incorporated as a town back in 1889. Ed and Ellen took on the task of hiring vendors to provide some food and drinks to those visiting. They spent the last half of October reaching out to companies in the neighborhood and were able to get more gracious responses than they expected.

Every painting that Amanda completed was placed in a fine frame purchased at Annie's Art and Frame shop, and a modest suggested price tag was attached. The museum suggested that the three best paintings be auctioned and said that the auctioneer could select an appropriate starting point based on how sales of the other paintings had gone.

The night before the event, the family of three huddled together and discussed the plan.

When Ellen was finished explaining who would do what, Amanda said, "You and Dad are doing all the work. I wish there was something I could do."

"Honey, you already did your work. You painted all of these." Ed's hand swept around the room at all the paintings surrounding them.

"I know. It's not like I can get up and make a speech or anything. You and Mom are the only ones who can understand me. I can't talk straight when half my mouth is frozen shut."

"You do fine, dear," Ellen replied.

"You lie so well, Mom," Amanda said, triggering a half smile on both of them.

After a few moments of silence, Amanda said, "What will we do if no one shows up?"

Ellen gulped. Ed came back strong. "They'll come. If you paint it, they will come. Right? Isn't that the way the saying goes?"

Amanda nodded and laughed in her own special way.

Growing serious, her father said, "Honey, we've put out flyers. The museum has their usual patrons that will be alerted when they are in the museum about your exhibit. We've got family and friends coming. I even invited some local celebrities. They'll be fighting over your paintings."

"Mom, Dad, thanks for helping me. I know we won't sell my paintings for a lot, but if we could get a few thousand to send to the researchers, that'd be something, right? That might help a little bit. I mean, I hoped to get twenty or thirty thousand, but I know that probably won't happen. Some of the dreary day sunsets won't even sell. And after we pay for the food services, we won't have much left to send, will we?"

"Anything," Ellen answered quickly. "Honey, anything helps. The research folks might be this close"— she held her right thumb and forefinger a quarter inch apart—"and your dollars might push them over the top."

A somber Amanda nodded. "I know. I just...I just hoped I could make a real difference."

Before their daughter expressed something too close to the fears they held themselves, Ed stood up, stretched, and said, "Big day tomorrow. I need to get my sleep."

That was Ellen's cue to begin helping Amanda prepare for bed.

At two o'clock on November third, the doors to the meeting room were opened. A bar was set up at the corner, manned by Tom Beck from Olaf's. Various pastries, sweets, and coffees were available in the opposite corner, at a table manned by Beth from Café Besalu.

By two fifteen, more than a dozen people wandered through the room gazing at the array of Ballard sunsets. By two thirty, it was more than twice that many. Upon entering, Ellen handed every person a one-page summary of Amanda's life and challenges and the story behind the paintings. The research foundation that she had selected was detailed on the flip side.

A man and woman came in together, and Ellen reached out to them with her flyer. "Welcome," she said.

The woman wore an elegant light blue dress with a faint flower print. The man was handsome and seemingly couldn't take his eyes off the woman.

"Thank you. I'm Amy. This is Rick. Which way should we go?"

Ellen pointed toward the bar and said, "You could get yourselves a beverage and then start with the first sunset, painted on September first. They're all in order with the last one, painted September thirtieth, at the far end."

Amy and Rick nodded their thanks and headed toward the bar. Arriving in line, they stood behind Jodi, who turned and said, "You look great in that dress, Amy! Wherever did you get that?"

Laughing, Amy looked at Rick and said, "Jodi is kidding. She knows I bought it at her store moments before I bumped into you."

Jodi laughed too. "Kind of magical, huh?"

Two old men, Alex and Martin, stared at the September seventh painting, and Martin said, "I like this one. Three hundred dollars doesn't seem like much."

"Oh, yeah," Alex replied. "Let's see you pull out a wad of hundreds and buy that bad boy then."

"You think I couldn't?"

"You're all talk. You even complain that coffee is too expensive," Alex countered.

Martin fumed a bit. "I'm just saying, three hundred isn't much for a nice piece of art. A cup of coffee lasts a half hour or so. This lasts forever."

"Well, you got the money?"

"No. But I've got a credit card. And I think I'm kind of an artist too. That little gal over there painted her heart out on this one. Least I can do is use my brilliant artistic skills to turn that three into an eight. What do you say, you got a pen?"

Alex handed his friend a ballpoint, and Martin bent over and altered the price on the three-by-five card taped to the wall next to it. He took it over to where Ed and his daughter sat behind a table with a cash box and a credit card machine.

"I want to buy this Seventh of September painting for eight hundred dollars," Martin said, glancing over at the artist.

Amanda reached over with her left hand and tugged her father's coat. Shaking her head, she mumbled something to him.

Her father looked at Martin and said, "Must be some mistake. Number seven is only three hundred dollars."

Martin shook his head. "You're right. There was a mistake. You made it when you priced it too low. What do you think, young lady, shall we send eight hundred to the research folks instead of three hundred?"

Straining to flash the straightest smile she could muster, Amanda nodded her agreement.

Martin handed over his card, and a line of people began to line up behind him.

Techie Cort Linley bought a brooding and dark September eighteenth painting.

Newly employed Will Hardesty and his wife, Denise, paid four hundred dollars for September third's depiction of the sunset.

Budding literary superstar Maury Woods ponied up seven hundred for a beautiful rendering of the sunset on September twenty-third.

A local celebrity, radio talk-show host, Dori Monson was next in line. He bought the September ninth sunset, offering a thousand dollars for it, four hundred more than the price tag showed. Ed accepted his payment and smiled back at him. "Thanks, Dori. I never miss your show and I thought you might want to stop by and revisit these mean streets of Ballard." Monson laughed, gave a nod to Amanda, and moved aside for the next purchaser.

As the line grew and more paintings sold, Ellen pulled her husband aside and asked, "What's going on? Some of these people are volunteering to pay more than the stated price."

"I don't know, but let's get what we can for her. I've got to get back; the next buyer is here already." Ed moved back to the counter and took another credit card from another buyer.

Every painting sold but one of the darkest, least attractive sunsets. Finally, the three that Amanda identified as her favorites were put up for verbal auction. A friend of Ed's from work was standing by. He had called auctions before at schools and charity events and agreed to manage this one for his friend.

The first painting was from September nineteenth. It featured swirling clouds and a gorgeous sunset that seemed unending. Amanda named it *Battle of Beauty*. Sarah Ahlberg and Wade Ibsen made the final and winning bid at eighteen hundred dollars. Accepting the painting, Wade said, "We've got a huge empty wall in the apartment and it'll look great there. Thank you, Amanda!"

Carrying it back to where Sarah stood, he said, "So I guess the payments on my student loan will have to be smaller for a while. Someday that'll be finished, but this painting is forever."

Sarah pecked him on the cheek. "Kinda like us, huh?"

"Exactly like us," Wade confirmed.

The second auctioned painting was from September tenth. It was a very rainy day, and at the end, a few weak rays of sunlight streamed through the clouds, fighting their way through as if to say, "We aren't done yet—don't shut us out." Amanda called this one *Unrelenting Hope*. Margaret and Heidi teamed up to bid the painting to over two thousand dollars, but Jason Lindberg pushed it further to over thirty-five hundred before giving up the fight. Holden Russell and his new wife, Kay, bought the painting with a final bid of four thousand dollars.

Finally, they arrived at the last painting to be sold by auction. In the back of the room, a tall man in a long gray trenchcoat, stood by, admiring the dark, unsold painting as the auction began.

Amanda had mixed feelings about selling this one. Her last one. Perhaps the last one she'd ever paint. She had named it *Leif's Sunset*. Her left hand and arm were twitching more now, and she felt certain that, barring a miracle, her painting days were short-lived. This last painting had a special meaning for her—one that gave her hope for the future.

The bidding started at one thousand and had crashed the five-thousand-dollar barrier within three minutes.

The auctioneer called it out. "Five thousand, do I hear six? Look at this painting, ladies and gentlemen. Absolutely spellbinding. I can hardly take my eyes off it. This is the sunset to top all sunsets in Ballard, and you can have it hanging on your living room wall!"

"Six thousand!" a woman yelled out, holding her paddle high.

Sixty seconds later, Mindy Byers raised her paddle and, doublechecking her checkbook totals one more time, said, "Nine thousand, seven hundred, and fifty dollars!"

The room grew silent.

The auctioneer said, "Do I hear ten thousand?"

Still more silence.

"Nine thousand, seven hundred, and fifty dollars going once. Going twice." Pausing for effect, the auctioneer raised his gavel and prepared to bring it down.

The lone man in the back of the room raised his paddle and walked forward. "Ten thousand!" he called out.

Mindy slumped back in her chair.

Every eye in the house turned to the man. No one recognized him.

He turned around and pointed to the lone, unsold painting. Pointing to it, he said, "I'll pay ten thousand dollars for that painting on the wall."

Before the auctioneer could remind him they were bidding on the painting at the front of the room, the man spoke again.

"And I'll pay two hundred thousand dollars for *Leif's Sunset*."

Every mouth in the room fell open. Half of them let out an elongated gasp.

The auctioneer's gavel resounded throughout the room. "Sold!" he yelled out. "Both paintings."

Amanda looked at her mom and a thousand tears rolled out of her eyes.

The man came forward to the table where their meager cash box and credit card machine sat, waiting for their biggest challenge yet.

"My name is Francis Delaney. I've been rather fortunate in my life, and it brings me great joy to spread some of that good fortune around." Looking directly at Amanda, he said, "And you, young lady, have done a miraculous job painting all this beauty. That one, that dark, lonely sunset—I like that one a lot. I really want that one for my own. And if I'm not wrong, I bet *Leif's Sunset* was your favorite too, right?"

Struggling for words, Amanda just nodded.

The man smiled. "I like it too. Who wouldn't? But it's that dark one that captivates me, so I was wondering if you would keep this beautiful bright one for me since I have nowhere to put it right now. Keep it in your room to remind you every day of what power you have to make a difference. Would you do that for me?"

Speaking now, because as anguished and fractured as it sounded, she knew she had to say something, Amanda said, "Yes. Thank you. Thank you so much."

Looking at Ed, Francis said, "I'll call and have my banker issue a cashier's check for two hundred and ten thousand and courier it over here. Should be here in thirty minutes or so. If you wouldn't mind, I'd like to sit and talk to Amanda some more. I'd like to understand how one person can have such a resilient and stout spirit."

Nodding his approval, almost too vigorously, Ed agreed.

Francis came around, pulled up a chair next to Amanda, and said, "Ballard is a pretty nice place to live, huh?"

Amanda, eyes wide in awe, nodded her answer.

"Amanda, I know speaking is hard. My dad had a stroke, and for him, it was his *left* side that wouldn't cooperate. I spent years talking with him, so I have a good ear for it. So will you talk with me?"

Again Amanda began to nod, then, thinking differently, she muttered, "Yes."

"Good," Francis said. "Tell me, Amanda. How did you summon the strength to do something as amazing as this?"

Amanda stared at him, blinking back her own tears. "I got no quit in me. I just don't want to give up."

As she wiped her eyes, her attention was diverted to the middle of the room where her parents were accepting congratulations on the successful event. She took the opportunity to lean a bit farther toward Francis and, in something akin to a conspiratorial whisper, Amanda said, "My parents worry about me. They think I paint sunsets because I feel I'm at my end."

Francis listened carefully and was certain he understood her correctly. "Are you? At the end, I mean."

"No," Amanda replied strongly. She paused a moment, then added, "I'm like Ballard."

Perplexed at that, Francis said, "I'm not sure I understand. How are you like Ballard?"

Amanda locked eyes with him and, still whispering, said, "Ballard has evolved and changed a lot, and some people think it'll always be just as it is now. They think *this* is the end product. Most people look at me and think I'm at the end too. But they don't know—I'm like Ballard. I'm just getting started."

## THE END

# My thanks to all
## the companies that participated:

**Ballard Bar & Grill (Ballard Bros.)** 5305 15th Ave NW 206-784-4440 ballardbrothers.com – More than just seafood, the newly renovated Ballard Bar and Grill now serves seafood, a large Tex-Mex menu and a brand new full bar area.

**Café Besalu** 5909 24th Ave NW 206-789-1463 Cafebesalu.com – Croissants, sweet & savory pastries, quiche & coffee served in a simple shop with a few tables.

**Gold Dogs** 5221 Ballard Ave NW 206-499-1811 Shopgolddogs.com – Eclectic clothing store showcasing a variety of new, vintage & repurposed fashions & leather goods.

**Hattie's Hat** 5231 Ballard Ave NW 206-784-0175 Hatties-hat.com – Hattie's Hat is a Ballard institution that has been around since 1904.Offering classic feel good American food for breakfast, lunch, dinner, and brunch. Located on Ballard Avenue, this long standing classic is never one to miss.

**Landmark** 5433 Leary Way NW 206-782-4000 gencarelifestyle.com/senior-living/wa/seattle – Ballard Landmark gives residents the opportunity to lead active, healthy lives. Sitting in the heart of vibrant Ballard lets residents participate in local events such as the Ballard Art Walk and Seafood Fests. Every Sunday, you can step outside to the Farmer's Market. Ballard Landmark is your destination for a safe and fun community.

**Lemon Drop Boutique** 5818 24th Ave NW 206-547-1840 facebook.com/Lemon-Drop-Boutique-184504700422/ – Lemon Drop is a swanky, vintage inspired boutique owned by Jodi Obde. The store is overflowing with fabulous finds, both old and new. We opened our doors in 2009 and we were soon voted, "Best New Boutique" in Seattle Magazines, Reader's Choice Awards!!

**Lockspot Tavern** 3005 NW 54th St. 206-789-4865 www.facebook.com/TheLockspotCafe – Rustic tavern for an array of classic American fare from omelets to fish n' chips with a full bar.

**Merrill Gardens** 2418 NW 56th St. 206-965-9370 Merrillgardens.com – Every day is an opportunity to celebrate your independence at Ballard, a Merrill Gardens senior living community in Seattle, WA. Your community is designed to meet your individual needs so you can experience the freedom to be yourself. Enjoy exceptional senior living from a family-owned company that knows connection is everything.

**Mike's Chili Parlor** 1447 NW Ballard Way 206-782-2808 – Tiny, low-key family-owned eatery and bar serving burgers, hot dogs & its signature chili since 1922.

**Monster Art and Clothing** 5000 20th Ave NW 206-789 0037 Monsterartandclothing.com – Monster: Art, Clothing & Gifts proudly features a wide variety of independent artists. Don't like art? Well, you probably wear socks and we've got a !#%& load of those.

**Nordic Museum** 2655 NW Market St. 206-789-5707 Nordicmuseum.org – We share Nordic culture with people of all ages and backgrounds by exhibiting art and objects, preserving collections, providing educational and cultural experiences, and serving as a community gathering place.

**Olaf's Bar** 6301 24th Ave NW 206-297-6122 Olafsballard.com – We are a Ballard bar that celebrates our diverse neighborhood by offering a selection of rotating beers and liquors, preparing fantastic food featuring local ingredients, and fostering long term relationships with our regulars, while having as much fun as is legally possible.

**Palermo Pizza & Pasta** 2005 NW Market St. 206-297-2728 Palermorestaurant.com – Solid food, beer and wine. Breakfast delivered, pizza and pasta, great service.

**Secret Garden Books** 2214 NW Market St. 206-789-5006 Secretgardenbooks.com – Veteran independent bookstore stocking titles for adults, kids, as well as hosting literary events.

**Sip and Ship** 1752 NW Market St. 206-789-4488 Sipandship.com – Small coffee, tea & snack spot with packaging, shipping & printing services plus cards and gifts.

**St. Alphonsus Church** 5816 15th Ave NW 206-784-6464 Stalseattle.org – St. Alphonsus Parish has been serving area Catholics, and the Seattle neighborhood of Ballard for over 100 years.

**Twice Sold Tales** 2419 NW Market St. 206-545-4226 Twicesoldtales.info – Specializing in rare, used, and out of print books, with an emphasis on fiction, Twice Sold Tales is moving soon to 1708 NW Market in the International Orders of Odd Fellows Hall. Books, cats, and mayhem!

# Didn't find your company in this book?

There are a lot of unique and interesting places in Ballard that I haven't visited yet or didn't find a way to work into a short story plot this time around. If you would like to be in a sequel to *Short Stories of Ballard*, email me at gary@smallbizsherpa.com and I will start working on the next edition.

# Gary Brose is also the author of:

*Bonus Your Way to Profits* (2008) – A step-by-step guide to creating radical change in your business's compensation structure. Stop paying people for simply showing up and punching in. Change your pay structure to a pay-for-performance model that rewards employees on a monthly basis for improving the quality of their work. Learn how to create a more motivated crew whose personal goals are aligned with the company goals in such a way that leads to a three-way win: the employee is more fairly rewarded for good work; the company gains an equal or greater value compared to the cost of the bonus plan; and, most importantly, the customers receive an improved service or product.

*The Ultimate Motivated Employee* (2012) – Written as an easy-to-read and thought-inspiring analysis of the seven keys to superior employee management. This is the book entrepreneurs and first-time managers need to read before they adopt a fatally flawed management style. Learn the seven keys to creating a fully motivated and engaged workforce that eventually learns how to lead itself, allowing management to get out of the way and watch as their employees become a super-charged crew. For every manager who believes he or she can bring out the full potential of their employees, *The Ultimate Motivated Employee* gives you the blueprint for making that happen.

*How to Get a Raise* (2015) – Written for the employees, not the managers, *How to Get a Raise* helps entry-level workers understand more about business and how they can be the masters of their own fate in the business world. Learn the seven steps to a higher paycheck and lose any fear you have of ever having to survive at minimum wage. Learn how to make yourself so valuable to your boss that job security is a given and advancement is inevitable. A great book for high school grads venturing out into the real world.

*Express Exec – A novel approach to outrunning the pace of change* (2018) – Are you a business owner, CEO, or manager in charge of a department? Inevitably, you will have to make serious and significant changes within your company or department that affect the employees. Since virtually everyone on the planet hates change with a passion, you can expect massive resistance to any changes you propose.

But the fact is the world is changing quickly, and those companies that don't adapt will fail. Sooner or later, you will have to make adjustments to duties, staffing, or, heaven forbid, pay rates! How do you do that?

That was the question that Andrea Lane faced. She is the fictional protagonist in *Express Exec* who must increase productivity dramatically within six months in order to save the company. You see, *Express Exec* is like no other business book you've ever read. **It is a business lesson buried in a novel**. The author wrote it that way so readers could put themselves into Andrea's shoes and "live" the transformation process that her department needs to go through. Sit in on management strategy sessions and group and one-on-one conversations between management and the employees. Experience, first-hand, the angst, fear, anger, and confusion as the employees try to grasp what the changes mean to them personally. When you are done reading *Express Exec*, you'll feel like you lived it and will better understand what steps *you* have to take to create a motivated and engaged workforce that embraces change rather than resists it.

******

For more information or to contact the author, visit
www.smallbizsherpa.com